# Beauty

## and the

# Serpent

# Beauty and the Serpent

## Thirteen Tales of Unnatural Animals

by **Barbara Ann Porte**

wood engravings by **Rosemary Feit Covey**

SIMON & SCHUSTER BOOKS FOR YOUNG READERS

New York • London • Toronto • Sydney • Singapore

for P. F.
my love and my mainstay
—B. A. P.

for Adam
—R. F. C.

SIMON & SCHUSTER BOOKS FOR YOUNG READERS
An imprint of Simon & Schuster Children's Publishing Division
1230 Avenue of the Americas, New York, New York 10020

Text copyright © 2001 by Barbara Ann Porte
Illustrations copyright © 2001 by Rosemary Feit Covey

The text for this book is set in Cg Cloister.
The illustrations are wood engravings.

Printed in the United States of America
2 4 6 8 10 9 7 5 3 1

Library of Congress Cataloging-in-Publication Data
Porte, Barbara Ann.
Beauty and the serpent : thirteen tales of unnatual animals / by Barbara Ann Porte ;
p. cm.
Summary: An eccentric school librarian tells offbeat stories involving fantastic animals and
encourages teachers and students to relate their own stories as well.
ISBN 0-689-84147-7
1. Children's stories, American. 2. Supernatural—Juvenile fiction.
[1. Supernatural—Fiction. 2. Animals—Fiction. 3. Storytelling—Fiction. Short stories.]
I. Covey, Rosemary Feit, 1954– ill. II. Title
PZ7.P776 Be 2001
[Fic]—dc21          00-046399

"What giants?" said Sancho Panza. "Those . . . are not giants, but windmills. . . ."

"It is clear," answered Don Quixote, "that thou art not experienced in the business of adventures. They are giants; and if thou art afraid, get thee aside and pray, whilst I engage with them in fierce and unequal battle."

*The Adventures of Don Quixote de la Mancha*
by Miguel de Cervantes

# Contents

# Dear Old Golden Rule Days

## (An Introduction of Sorts)

Welcome to the Ernestine Wilde Alternative High School! Its focus is on independent learning. There are hardly any rules. Yet every day plenty of students manage to break them. Then they get sent to the library.

"Do your teachers think I'm running a jail?" grumbles Ms. Lavinia Drumm, head librarian. "Find a book! Take a seat! Learn something!" she tells them. The students do, though it's seldom, if ever, what the teachers intended.

"So long as she keeps them out of my hair, who cares? Didn't she used to be a gypsy storyteller?" they ask one another. They mean "itinerant." Ms. Drumm traveled, but that was long ago. Now she's getting on in years. Even so, I'd say she looks more than fit for a caravan: Six foot one in stocking feet, she's broad-shouldered and large-breasted, but otherwise slim, with high-boned, ruddy cheeks, a long nose, full lips, and a strong, dimpled chin. Her gray hair is frizzled and thick, and worn down to her shoulders. Her exotic good looks are accentuated by the clothes she wears: floor-length dark skirts, French-cuffed silk shirts, high-top laced shoes, and voluminous shawls in bright colors that she frequently drapes over backs of chairs to keep out of her way. No less eccentric is her jewelry: plasticine pendants in the shape of shrunken skulls or disembodied eyes; long necklaces whose links resemble bones; serpentine bracelets with ruby fangs and faces; and an assortment of strange rings. It's enough to give even an adolescent pause; and it does.

Finding themselves the object of Ms. Drumm's steely stare, her cerulean eyes disconcertingly enlarged behind half-reading glasses, and one slightly off center; or hearing themselves addressed in her low-pitched, mysterious voice, students pay attention. Let one of them take too long and Ms. Drumm will bang her stick on the floor. It's a carved wooden crook she carries for balance on account of a long-standing foot problem. Its handle is decorated with animal heads. She calls the stick her shillelagh. She's banging it now.

# A Doggish Tale

Marlene looks up. ("Pronounce it Mar-lay'-na," she's forever telling people.) Marlene's orange hair is styled in spikes. They stick out perfectly all over her head, precisely perpendicular to her scalp. The lipstick she has on today is black, or possibly purple. Little gold and silver rings are attached to her nose, one of her eyebrows, her ear rims and lobes. Her jaws are moving furiously.

Though Ms. Drumm would outlaw body piercing if she could, all she tells Marlene now is: "Feet on the floor, please! Sit up straight! There's no chewing in the library. Get rid of the gum!" Marlene swallows it.

"Eat gum and your insides will stick together. Your rectum will close up. Didn't your mother ever tell you that?" Ms. Drumm asks Marlene. Rectum? Did the librarian actually say "rectum"?

Momentarily, Marlene is speechless. Then, regaining her composure, she says, "Right! Swallow a watermelon seed and a watermelon

tree will grow in your stomach. Anything you pick up off the ground and put into your mouth for sure will poison you. I stopped believing all of that when I gave up Santa Claus."

"I see," says Ms. Drumm. "But you know just because one story isn't so doesn't mean another can't be. Take poisoning, for instance. Not that long ago, and in this neighborhood, there was a most peculiar case. Listen," she says. Then, sitting atop the table beside Marlene's, Ms. Drumm begins:

Once, on a dreary and overcast day, a teenage girl was pushing a little boy in his stroller. Baby-sitting that afternoon, she'd timed their excursion wrong. Therefore, while they were out it had begun to drizzle, really just a fine mist, but nevertheless unpleasant. Also, she'd walked too far, so that by now it was well past time for the baby's snack. On top of which, she'd forgotten to take along the diaper bag packed with the baby's toys, juice, and crackers. The usually pleasant baby was fussing. Soon he began crying full force, which may help to explain what happened next.

Increasingly out-of-sorts herself, and feeling somewhat put-upon, the teenage girl had just wheeled the stroller with the shrieking baby in it under an overpass. It was not quite a tunnel, but almost. As they emerged, she saw, lying nearly at the edge of the sidewalk, a tan-colored pacifier, the sort you stick into babies' mouths to comfort them and make them be quiet. Only the tip of its squared-off handle and the edge of its circular shield were in contact with the pavement. Its plump, rounded nipple was sticking up, enticingly, at a forty-five-degree angle from the ground. Though not wrapped, the pacifier looked brand-new, as though, perhaps, it had fallen from some baby carriage before ever being used.

Just like that, the girl bent over, picked it up and, wiping the nipple on her jacket sleeve, popped it into the baby's mouth. How she could have done so, I'll never know. Immediately, though, the baby stopped crying and began to suck happily. He went on sucking all the way home and, once there, was reluctant to give up the pacifier even for food. Afterward, that pacifier became the baby's favorite possession, and he never willingly went anywhere without it. Nor would a substitute satisfy. Even well past the pacifier stage, he held on tightly to that one.

"It looks ridiculous in such a big boy's mouth," his mother frequently told him. Yet what could she do? From being a pleasant baby, her child had turned into a wild thing with a mind of his own, a terrible temper, a piercing howl, and very sharp teeth. To try to take that pacifier away was to risk being bit. How embarrassing!

"I guess that's why they call it the terrible twos," his mother said, shamefaced, to the baby-sitter.

"Ummm," said the baby-sitter, neatly sidestepping her unruly charge. He hadn't always been this way. She remembered to the day when his badness had started. Now just the sight of his pacifier made her uncomfortable. Whatever had possessed her to pick it up so blithely and put it in his mouth? Also, she was astonished to see it still looked brand-new. How was that possible?

Pausing briefly now, the librarian looks around. A small group of students have gathered to listen. She fixes her eyes on each in turn. "I'll tell you how. Remarkable though it may be, what's made in the devil's workshop comes with a lifetime guarantee. Well, I can see that you're skeptical. I'm not surprised. Why would sensible students like you believe in witchcraft, or in sorcery, or in spells? Yet think how many stories through the centuries abound with them. Have you never considered that at least one or two might be true? Maybe not. Most of us don't—until someone, or something, comes along to change our minds. Perhaps a puppy from hell. . . .

"Ah, you smile; but believe me, now and then when the devil is bored, just to see what will happen, he sends such a puppy up into the world. Woe to families that take them in! 'It's a puppy from hell,' desperate owners say afterward to anyone who will listen. Certainly that was the case with the dog in this story." Then, giving a long, drawn-out sigh, Ms. Drumm continues to tell it:

The puppy arrived one day in a downpour, sucking its bubba, which is what pacifiers were called where it came from. Alas, soon after, it dropped it somewhere. Whimpering over its lost possession, the puppy huddled beneath a tree, shivering. The climate was considerably colder up here than below.

Eventually, a spry grandmother out for exercise came loping along. She was dressed in rain clothes and carrying an open umbrella. Seeing the bedraggled puppy, she took pity on it and popped it into an oversized, waterproof coat pocket. Back home, she told both her husband and his mother, who lived with them, "I've found the perfect pet to keep us company in our retirement, and also to entertain the grandchildren when they visit." But of course she hadn't. That puppy grew like a weed. In almost no time it was standing on tables, sprawling on furniture, knocking over lamps, grabbing food from everyone's plate, chewing shoes and whatever else was around and, in between, barking excessively. Also, it drooled.

"It's a puppy from hell," the despairing woman told friends and relatives.

"Maybe it's just in need of professional training," dog owners among them advised. Fortunately, a canine obedience school was nearby. The woman registered her pet for a beginner course, then took it twice a week for lessons. The dog did very well in school, even earning a diploma to hang on the wall alongside pictures of the couple's grandchildren; but it continued misbehaving at home exactly as before.

"Perhaps it has worms, or some sort of nervous condition," the woman's husband suggested. The woman took it to the veterinarian.

"This puppy needs worming, or else tranquilizers," she said, certain herself by now it was the latter.

"Oh, no," the veterinarian said, having examined the puppy briefly. "Very healthy animal, only high-strung, probably suffering pangs of insecurity. Very common problem among recovering strays. We're using drugs only as a last resort. Best first to try counseling." The veterinarian gave the woman a business card by way of referral. DR. SO AND SO, CANINE PSYCHOLOGIST. "Very capable, very busy. You may have to wait some months for an appointment," she warned.

Back home, feeling a bit high-strung and insecure herself, the woman slept poorly. All night she thought she heard the sounds of someone, or something, stealthily gnawing. She didn't have the heart to investigate. In the morning she discovered the puppy had chewed up the last of the kitchen chair legs so that everyone wobbled at breakfast, except for a visiting grandchild who still used a high chair, entirely chrome plated. The woman telephoned her own physician and made an appointment.

"You're my last hope," she said, and explained her situation: "I've grandchildren galore, in and out the door; my decrepit mother-in-law lives with me; and, as you can see, I'm no spring chicken myself. Now

I've got this puppy from hell. I'd give it away, but no one will take it. The veterinarian said to try counseling. You have to help me. I'm at the end of my rope."

"Umm," murmured the physician, who could see that it was so, and also was aware the woman's health insurance plan did not include counseling. Therefore, she gave her a prescription for tranquilizers. "Come see me in a year," she told her.

"Thank you," said the woman. She had the prescription filled, went home, and fed the puppy four pills. Almost right away they started working. The dog stopped standing on tables, grabbing from plates, chewing shoes and furniture, and barking excessively. It also no longer drooled, dry mouth being a side effect of the medicine. It did sometimes still sprawl, though now very peaceably, on the living-room sofa, but as the sofa was old, the woman didn't mind.

"The puppy from hell is turning out fine," she told everyone.

"It's the lessons," said the trainer.

"It's the therapy," said the veterinarian.

"It's growing up," said the woman's mother-in-law.

"Ummm," said the woman, and smiled, sphinxlike, at them all.

Ms. Drumm stops speaking to clear her throat.

"But what happened to the baby?" someone asks.

"I'm just coming to that part," the librarian replies:

Down in hell, the devil wondered that, too. Therefore, early one morning he came up into the world to peek in on the family and see for himself. Oh, my! No longer a baby, that boy had grown by leaps and bounds. "Like a weed," his father said. It was almost as though his son had undergone a metamorphosis. Uncommonly gangly, wild and disorderly, the boy knocked over lamps, stood on the furniture, wolfed down his food and, when he didn't get his way, howled raucously. He was doing all of it this moment, knowing it would make him late for school. How it warmed the devil's heart to see such pandemonium.

And there was more. Following the boy into his bedroom, the devil watched him as he dressed. How weird! From head to toe, the boy's body was fuzzy, and despite his tender years wiry hair was already sprouting in private places; his arms and his legs were unnaturally furry. Sometime back his mother had noticed this, too. She'd made an appointment with the pediatrician. "Is there something wrong with my son?" she asked.

"Precocious puberty," said the physician. "It's nothing to worry about. A slight imbalance in hormones that in a few years will all straighten out. Believe me, it's traumatic only for mothers."

"But he's only a baby. He still takes his pacifier to bed," said *this* mother.

"Ah," the doctor said, and looked serious. "Immature attachment to nipple," he jotted in his records. Then, consulting his patient's medical plan, which was generous, he recommended counseling. Naturally, they tried it.

"The main thing is to reinforce good behavior through a system of rewards," the psychologist told them. "Bad behavior we ignore until it goes away." Nothing tickles the devil, or adolescents, more than such advice. Certainly, in this case, the outcome was predictable. In the first place, there was never any good behavior to reward; and in the second place, the bad behavior just got worse. Thus, by the time the devil arrived, things were out of hand entirely.

"A belt applied to his behind is what that boy needs," his father said. But his mother argued it would be against the law. So, instead, that very day, his father signed him up for golf lessons. It's a disciplined game played by gentlemen; surely some good will come of it, he reasoned.

*Clubs and hard balls, how appropriate,* thought the devil, and returned home to wait. He didn't have long.

The boy hated golf; whacking little white balls seemed pointless to him. Bored, he struck up friendships with sportsmen at the bar who admired his wildness. One day, having guzzled down some leftover drinks, that wild child jumped into a golf cart, took off at high speed, and crashed headlong into a tree.

You can imagine the grief and the mourning, the local headlines and the television coverage. "He was the sweetest baby you'd ever want to see," his mother kept saying. Afterward, she kept in a box, as mementos, his baby pacifier and his first pair of shoes, bronzed.

When the boy arrived in hell, the devil knew him right away. "I was expecting you," he said, and apprenticed him to the demon in charge of the devil's kennels.

"At first the boy was slovenly and snappish, but in almost no time the demon had him whipped into shape. Then, to reward his good behavior, the demon gave him a present. "Suck it," he said. "It will take away your cares and troubles. Down here we call it a 'bubba.'"

"Thank you," said the apprentice. Then, popping it into his mouth, he sucked happily. It had that same wild, sinful taste as his old one.

"My new acolyte is doing fine," the demon reported to the devil.

"I'm not surprised," the devil replied.

"Well, neither was I," says Ms. Drumm. Then, standing, stretching, reaching for her walking stick, she asks anyone for a lift home. "My van's in the shop," she tells them. Driver ed. is a popular course. Even some juniors have cars. Marlene volunteers. Once there, she helps Ms. Drumm carry book bags to her door. They're met by a barking dog. "It's my puppy from hell, but don't worry—it doesn't bite." Ms. Drumm nuzzles its face, and it licks her ear. Then, "Here!" she says, and tosses it a baby pacifier to play with. Unfortunately, given the circumstances of placement and lighting, whether chewed or brand-new, Marlene can't tell.

# Squirrel Aunty

Joseph and José have been sent to the library for fighting. They're still fighting. Ms. Drumm intervenes. "What's wrong with you two! You're acting like three-year-olds. How old are you, anyway?"

"Fourteen," says José.

"*Catorce,*" says Joseph, who is in his first year of Spanish and failing it. He hardly ever turns in any homework, though he almost always has an excellent excuse: The cat ate it. My brother threw up on it. We had a fire in our house.

"*Bueno* for you," says Ms. Drumm. "I remember being fourteen. It was terrible. My parents couldn't stand it. As soon as my summer vacation started, they took off for Australia and left me behind. Not that I wanted to go. I was sure at the time that Australia was one vast and uncivilized continent populated almost entirely by kangaroos. What I wanted to do was stay home on my own in the city. Instead, my parents sent me to visit my grandmother in the suburbs. How boring!"

"What did you do there?" José asks.

"What could I do?" Ms. Drumm replies. "No one my age seemed to live in the neighborhood, and my grandmother was ancient. She had long white hair rolled up into a bun, and wrinkled skin. I can still recall the jewelry she wore, antique and ornate; and her manner of dress was peculiar: long flowery skirts, faded T-shirts, white socks, and tennis shoes. Worst of all was the ruffled parasol she carried with her whenever she went out. Though others treated her with great respect, and often sought her advice, in my adolescent wisdom, I was embarrassed just to be seen with her."

"Where did the two of you go?" Joseph asks.

"Nowhere! Haven't you been listening?" Ms. Drumm frowns. "It's true that at first my grandmother tried hard to think of projects to engage me, but as I made it clear from the start that I didn't care to go walking with her, or weed herbal beds, or help maintain her records of local butterflies, she soon came to leave me alone. After the first week she addressed me directly only when necessary. I kept count of the days before I would leave. Perhaps so did she. Then, not long before the end of my stay, she told me something extraordinary."

"What?" ask both boys.

"Be still, and I'll tell you," says Ms. Drumm. Taking a seat atop one of the desks, she begins:

I remember perfectly how gloomy it was that day, the air heavy with mist and threatened rain. Sitting at the kitchen table, having just finished breakfast, I stared through a fogged-up window into the yard, feeling sorry for myself. My attention was caught, first by the chittering and fluttering of various small birds eating from a feeder, next by a pair of large, shrieking black birds, then finally by several squirrels dashing madly about. With my eyes, I followed an especially frantic one that appeared to be searching desperately, racing from one unmarked spot to another, anxiously digging. As one who often misplaced things, frequently items needed for school—a pencil, a notebook, some signed piece of paper—you might think I would have felt some sympathy for that squirrel. But, no. Instead, "Look at that stupid squirrel," I muttered.

My grandmother looked. So did Esme, a woman even older than my grandmother, who'd worked most of her life in my grandmother's house. She still came twice a week, on Tuesdays and on Thursdays, to iron and to cook. They kept each other company.

Esme laughed. "That must be some sort of squirrel person," she said. "I know just how it feels. 'Now where did I put that acorn?' it's asking itself. 'I thought for sure I left it here, or there, or maybe over there.'"

"Why not?" said my grandmother. "When all is said and done, it's no different from us—always looking for something that's missing." She glanced my way as she spoke.

Squirrel person, indeed! How stupid can they be? I smirked deliberately. My grandmother regarded me curiously, or perhaps with displeasure, for several moments. Then, addressing me directly, she asked, "Have you ever heard of reincarnation?"

"Of course," I replied. "It's something that people who don't know better believe in. They think after we die, we come back."

"Yes, it's true," said my grandmother, leaving me to wonder if she meant that I'd got the answer right, or meant that we truly come back. "But not always as a person," she added. "Some say it depends on the kind of life one has led. I know of such a case." She seated herself across from me.

At that, Esme untied her apron and also sat, but on my side of the table and facing my grandmother. She waited, expectantly. For a long moment no one said anything. My grandmother pursed her lips, drew her thick eyebrows together, and seemed to be gathering her thoughts. Then, looking straight at me, she said, "Listen."

Squirrel Aunty was what everybody called her: the children, their parents, other adults who lived in the neighborhood, several blocks of apartment houses that lined the boulevard. The buildings were old, even dilapidated, but they still showed signs of their former elegance: wrought-iron doorways, for instance, marble steps, and real crystal chandeliers in the lobbies, everything always in need of cleaning and polishing.

Squirrel Aunty herself was old, and dilapidated. As long as anyone could remember, she'd lived there. Daily she traversed the lobby, exiting the building and crossing the narrow access street, to sit alone on the same park bench, out of dozens that she could have picked. The benches were arranged in facing rows along the grassy, tree-shaded strips that ran up and down both sides of the boulevard. She always dressed the same—in a loose-fitting housecoat, with bedroom slippers on her feet. In cold weather she added heavy rag socks, and threw on a dark-colored overcoat. Wisps of long gray hair were forever escaping from her pinned-up bun. There she sat, day after day, talking to the squirrels, feeding them nuts and seeds, and goodness knows what, from a brown paper sack.

For the most part, neighborhood residents took her for granted and left her alone. Only young hooligans sometimes harassed her. These were children who ran from morning until night, unsupervised, along the boulevard, their boundaries arbitrarily set by a butcher shop to the east and a Greek Orthodox church to the west. The blocks in between they made their own—running, shouting, leaping, tossing balls, and rolling hoops, normal childhood behavior that tormented the old people who clustered up and down the boulevard, sitting on the benches, taking in the sun, playing card games or checkers, gossiping among themselves in several languages, none of them English. The boldest of these children would sometimes stand still, point at Squirrel Aunty, make faces, and whisper. Usually she ignored them; sometimes she made faces back, shook her fist, threw food. Then they'd call her a witch and run away, laughing.

"Is she really a witch?" children visiting from other neighborhoods would sometimes ask them.

"What do you think? Get a good look at her eyes, why don't you," was their usual reply. Then those who got close enough saw what they meant. Squirrel Aunty's eyes were truly peculiar, abnormally wide-set, protuberant, and beady. But, strangest of all, she had one eye that was blue and one that was brown. Yet for all that, she seemed to have excellent vision, and children coming eye to eye with her were quick to back away. Except for Marie.

Well, why not? Wasn't she different, too? A somewhat frail and gentle child, her eyes were fine, but she limped on account of one of her legs being shorter than the other. She'd had polio when she was five. Though she tried, it was hard for her to keep up with the others. Sometimes she sat beside Aunty on her bench and helped her feed the squirrels.

"Never mind," Aunty told her now and then. "Squirrels have short legs, too. Two short and two long, but see how well they manage." Once in a great while, when all the peanuts were gone, she'd reach into her housecoat pocket, take out an old penny, and give it to Marie.

"Witch money," the other children said when she showed them.

"No telling where it's been," their mothers whispered among themselves.

"I don't want you taking money from her," Marie's own mother told her. "Poor old woman; she needs every penny that she has. She's got no one and nothing."

"She's got a diamond ring," Marie said. "Isn't that something?" It was true that she did, and everyone knew it. In fact, it was a two-diamond ring; large, square, yellowish stones set side by side in heavy gold. She wore it every day—right hand, ring finger—dressing up her housecoat and her bedroom slippers. Sometimes she'd twist it on her finger as she sat there on the bench.

"Next time you're hungry, try eating a diamond ring," Marie's mother told her. But later Marie heard her mother talking with her father. "Someday someone's going to knock that old woman over the head and kill her, all for that diamond ring. You'd think she'd have sense enough to sell it."

But Marie knew why she didn't. "It's magic," she told the other children. "Anytime she wants, she only has to twist it on her finger and make a wish. Whatever she asks for comes true. Once, she let me touch it."

"Yah, so why doesn't she twist it and wish herself out of this dump?" asked one of the hooligans.

"Into a country palace, with good things to eat, fancy clothes, and new shoes," said another.

"She could take her squirrels with her," a third child added. "They'd like it in the country—lots more trees, and space to run."

"Hey, she could maybe even wish herself a squirrel," the first one said, speaking again. "Now wouldn't that be something? Squirrel

Aunty in a real squirrel fur coat living in a palace!" It was the start of winter when he said it.

Picturing Aunty in her own fur coat, Marie smiled. It would certainly be an improvement over what she had on. "It's a wonder that woman doesn't catch her death of cold, the way she dresses," Marie's mother said, seeing Aunty there when she called Marie in.

Even indoors it was cold that night. Wind whipped around the corners of buildings, rattling windows, blowing in through crevices around sashes and sills. Marie, snuggled beneath her covers, slept deeply, and dreamed. All night her dream was the same: She and Aunty were squirrels, living in a palace, racing up and down trees, running through fields and through woods. It was winter. Snow covered the ground, but didn't slow them down. On four perfect legs, Marie scampered everywhere with no problem.

How disappointed she must have been in the morning, awakening, climbing out of bed, limping, as usual, to the window to look out. But then, having wiped away the frost, what a sight met her eyes. Overnight, it truly *had* snowed. Wherever Marie looked, the world was covered in white. The effect was nearly blinding. And the snow continued to fall. It fell all that day and into the next; no ordinary storm, but a record-setting blizzard. Even after the flakes had stopped coming down, the wind went on blowing them into huge drifts, blocking sidewalks and doorways. Whoever could stay at home, did.

It wasn't until the morning of the third day that the sun came out, turning the boulevard into a shimmering byway. Trees looked as though hung with diamonds and pearls; rooftop cornices glistened. As ice began to melt from roofs and windows, icicles formed, soon to be broken off by children who licked them like Popsicles. People began emerging from buildings onto the streets, some heading for work, others just looking around, most of them bemoaning the weather. The children, though, were gleeful, tramping about, shouting, kicking up snow, shaping it into balls for throwing, rolling snowmen, a few lucky ones with metal-runnered wooden sleds in tow. They'd worry about school tomorrow. Only Squirrel Aunty was missing from the scene, that day, and the next, and the one after that. Her park bench stayed vacant, blanketed by snow, marked with tiny rodent footprints.

Why none of the mothers checked on her, perhaps the devil knows. They said, afterward, they'd been so busy—clearing away tracked-in slush, stuffing newspapers into window cracks, draping radiators with children's wet outer clothes, keeping hot soup simmering on the stoves. If they'd thought about Squirrel Aunty at all, it was only to be glad that she'd finally showed sense enough to stay in. It was the squirrels who acted worried; anxious and nervous. Maybe they were hungry; all that snow covering up their buried stores, and no one there to feed them.

The super said he'd never seen anything like it, the way those squirrels behaved: scolding on the fire escape outside her window, chattering in the stairwell, one frantic pair found riding the dumbwaiter, startling the couple who lived beneath her. That's why, the super explained, when Aunty didn't answer the doorbell and ignored his banging, he let himself in with his master key.

It was dark at first, and he couldn't see. But, oh, he said, it smelled awful! He pulled up the blinds and turned on a light. The door to the bedroom was open. Inside he could see a few squirrels, and a bump in the bed. He scattered the squirrels and examined the bump. It was the old woman, burrowed under a plaid comforter, dressed in a housecoat, slippers on her feet, her winter coat pulled around her. One close look and the super knew she was dead. That's when he backed out of the room, left the apartment, and ran down the stairs to find witnesses.

"Don't anyone touch anything," this one told that one. Somebody called the police. An ambulance came and removed Squirrel Aunty. "A case of hypothermia," said an attendant. The apartment was sealed. "Until her next of kin can be notified," said an officer. The neighbors thought she had no one. Eventually, though, a great-niece appeared, a deceased sister's granddaughter. Where had she been until now?

"Well, it's not as if I'm living in the neighborhood," she told a captain. She registered a claim for her aunt's diamond ring. "Two yellow stones set in gold," she described it. "A family heirloom said to be valuable." According to the police it hadn't turned up. Detectives questioned the super.

"You don't think I'd steal from the same dead body I found and reported, do you?" he asked. "She was a crazy old lady. For all I know she hid that ring, buried it, gave it to a squirrel. Sure, now that I think of it, it does seem to me I saw a squirrel running off with something shiny in its teeth. It could have been the ring."

"And I'm the king of France," said one of the detectives.

Among themselves, the neighbors speculated: Squirrel or super, which was more likely? But as time passed, talk faded. Somewhere Squirrel Aunty lay buried, in a family plot or a potter's field. Marie hoped there were trees there, and squirrels.

"Oh, there's sure to be," her mother told her.

So that would have been that—except for the rumors that began in the spring. First they had to do only with noisy squirrels. Agitated, said some. They seemed to be scurrying more than usual, and digging more frantically. "Those squirrels are crazy; keep your distance," mothers warned children. Among themselves, they talked about rabies. The children talked about witches and ghosts. One reported having seen a squirrel with a ring that glittered on its tail. Soon others reported seeing it, too. "Squirrel Aunty's spirit," they whispered.

Marie said nothing, but she listened, and watched, and bided her time. She took for her station Aunty's old bench. Day after day she sat and fed squirrels. She tossed them nuts and seeds and stale bread crumbs. She favored one—the grayest, fuzziest, chattiest one. Close and closer it came, climbed up beside her, took food from her fingers. To Marie it felt almost like old times. Afterward, she tried telling her mother: "I saw it with my own eyes. It's Aunty's ring on its tail—a diamond ring, two yellow stones, side by side, set in gold."

"Get on with you now," said her mother. "Well, maybe," she allowed when Marie persisted. She'd heard of pack rats stealing. Why not a squirrel? A ring on its tail began to seem possible.

But it was the butcher's boy, hearing talk about the ring, who made up his mind that spring to get it. He'd set a trap. He knew about rodent traps from the butcher shop. Of course this was different. For all he knew, this squirrel was witched, under a spell, or could cast one. Sorcery has its own rules. He visited the library, left with books tucked inside his shirt, took them home to study from. Then he built a wire cage. It was intended to capture, not meant to kill.

The night that he set it, there came a terrible storm; bolts of lightning, claps of thunder, water pouring from the sky in torrents. Afterward, some said lightning hit that trap and set it ablaze, that the falling rain put out the fire. If so, it fell too late for the squirrel. On the ground the next morning, those same people said, the butcher's boy found only the ring, its stones cracked, and the gold melted. Nothing else.

"Talk," said Marie's mother. "It's all just talk; pure speculation." Yet this much was true: No one ever saw the ring-wearing squirrel again, and that butcher's boy went mad—stark raving mad, as though possessed by the devil, or by his squirrel disciples. Wherever he went he saw squirrels—crouched in corners, peeking out from beneath furniture or from behind doors, balanced on ceiling meat hooks—beady eyes watching him. At night he felt them crawl on him—sharp teeth and claws puncturing his skin. He'd be awakened by the sounds of his own shrieking. Month after month this went on, until one morning that boy's body was found in the freezer room by the butcher. It was frozen stiff, a corpse, pressed against the farthest wall, as though trying to escape. Its skin was riddled by bite marks, jagged tears made by rodent teeth, and two of its fingers and three of its toes were missing.

"It was a terrible shame," said the butcher. "See what greed gets you in the end," parents warned children. "It was Squirrel Aunty come back from the dead to take back her ring," the children whispered to one another. "Aaagh, it's all just stories," Marie's mother said. Marie knew better. There was something she'd never told even her mother. That day on the bench, hand-feeding the squirrel, she'd stroked its tail, twisted the ring, and made a wish. Then the squirrel had bobbed its head, and Marie had seen both its eyes: One eye was blue, the other was brown.

"Amazing, isn't it?" says the librarian, looking around. Her circle of listeners has greatly increased.

"Is that the end?" one of them asks.

Ms. Drumm replies, "Not quite, but Esme, my grandmother's helper, *thought* that it was. 'Fantastic!' she said, shaking her head, rising from the table. Naturally, my grandmother agreed. 'Yes,' she said. Then, staring straight at me, she added, 'What was even more fantastic, though, was that not long afterward Marie began to lose her limp. By the time she was grown she walked as well as anybody—almost as well.' And that was the end of my grandmother's story."

Finished telling it, Ms. Drumm now reaches for her shillelagh. Carefully she stands, walks to her desk, and lowers herself onto her swivel chair. In twos and threes, the students drift off, back to their homerooms. School is nearly over for the day.

Presently, finding herself alone, Ms. Drumm does something she often does. Removing from her finger a ring she always wears, she twirls it on the desktop. It spins and spins, finally slows, falls over, and stops. That's when a person can see what sort of a ring it is: very old, made up of two cracked, yellow stones, set in a band of misshapen gold. *What a wonderful coincidence!* Joseph thinks, having returned to the room for his Spanish language notebook.

In MEMORY of
JED MARSTON
1716 ~ 1776

# Ghost Story

It's Halloween. Ms. Hall, the history teacher, has brought her entire class to the library to do research. "We're studying the Revolutionary War," she announces to Ms. Drumm. She tells the students, "I expect you all to work quietly on your own." Then, almost as an afterthought, she chirps brightly, "I'm just going to pop out for a bit. I won't be gone long. I'll be back momentarily." She's planning a visit to the teachers' lounge to have a cup of tea. She hopes it will settle her nerves. Hardly through the doorway, she complains to the teachers she finds there, "Those children have been acting like goblins all day."

Meanwhile, back in the library, Ms. Drumm is asking the class, "Who wants to hear a Revolutionary War story about a ghostly encounter?" Of course all of them do. "Then, listen," she says.

It was Halloween night in 1777 and a full moon was out when two soldiers whose company was camped north of Albany, New York, decided to borrow their captain's horse to go gambling. Riding bare-back and double, they headed for a place they knew in a pindling town a half dozen or so miles from where they were bivouaced. Taking the shortest route, they cut across the southwest corner of a cemetery.

"Yonder is old man Marston's grave," said the soldier mounted behind, his hands holding tight to the first one's waist. "Meanest man who ever lived, I've heard. Folk say now that he's dead you can call for him in any shape you want, and that's the way he'll come."

"Do you believe that?" asked the soldier in front.

"Nah, it's just a story."

"I don't believe it, either," said the first one. Then, to prove he truly meant it, he reined in the horse, leaned his knees into its withers to raise himself, and called, "Hey! You there! Old man Marston!" And he told the dead man he wanted him to come out with a head like a bulldog's, eyes like a frog's, body long as a fence rail, tail curled over him. After waiting a moment or two in the graveyard to see what would happen, he finally said, "Aagh, ain't nothing coming. Let's go."

"You're the one holding the reins," said the other. So they went on to town and commenced gambling.

They won some, lost some, ended up near even, and started back the way they had come, including taking the shortcut through the cemetery. As they were approaching that old man's grave, the first soldier saw something coming out of it; thought he did. But he didn't say anything. He just waited to see if the other had seen it. By the time that *thing* had got up alongside the horse, the second soldier said, "Hey, have a look! Do you see what I see? What is that?"

"I don't know, but I've been watching it," answered the first one. Then, pulling back on the reins, reaching for his rifle, he said, "I'm gonna shoot it."

"No you ain't, either," said the second one, grabbing hold of the gunstock. "You fire that gun, the sergeant will hear it. No questions

asked, he'll shoot us for sure. We've gotta pass right by his tent."
Already they could hear that sergeant's guard dog barking.

So the two soldiers rode on. And that *thing,* whatever it was, went right along with them: turned to the left, to the right, kept straight ahead, or stopped, just as they did. They had to cross a shallow stream, hardly a rivulet, and the horse splashed some, but that *thing* just jumped over it, then waited on the other side for them to catch up. Seeing that, again the first soldier reined in the horse and, reaching for his rifle, said, "Whatever that is, I'm gonna shoot it."

"No you ain't, either," the second one said, grabbing onto the gunstock the same as before. "Sure as you do, old sergeant'll shoot us." By now they could hear the sounds of the sergeant's guard dog headed full speed in their direction. So the soldiers took off, arms and legs wrapped around the captain's horse, it running as fast as it could with two on its back.

Ms. Drumm pauses. If a pin were to drop in the library this second, a person would hear it. Then, lowering her voice just a pitch, and speaking slowly, she brings her story to an end:

The way I heard it, those two never did shoot that thing, nor find out what it was. Afterward, they always claimed it had followed them most of the way back to the camp, until the sergeant's dog finally ran it off. The most those soldiers ever could say for sure was how it looked: a head like a bulldog's, eyes like a frog's, body long as a fence rail, its tail curled over it.

"Moon-colored," said one.

"Color of a tombstone," said the other.

"And that was that," says Ms. Drumm.

# Basement Imposter

Today is Friday. Ms. Drumm is not in the library. It's being supervised by a volunteer mom. "I'm off to Midwinter. It's a librarians' convention in Washington, D.C. I'll be back Monday," Ms. Drumm had told some of the students yesterday. By now, students seem to have taken over the room. For one thing they've rehung the sign Ms. Drumm usually keeps stored in her "miscellany closet," and puts up only when she's expecting a visit from outside dignitaries. MEDIA CENTER, it reads; and as though in confirmation, most of the students this moment are seated in front of computers, totally focused on electronic games. Except in one corner a group of girls are sprawled on floor mats, planning a slumber party. Not counting Aimee Yee, all of them are chewing gum.

"If we each bring our own sleeping bag, do you think we could have the party downstairs in your rec room?" Jolie asks her.

Aimee shakes her head. "Maybe upstairs," she says. "My mom would never let us stay overnight in the basement."

"Why not?" Selinda wants to know.

Aimee shrugs. "She once had some kind of weird experience." When pressed for details she adds, "All I know is what my mom's told me." Then, sitting up straight, adjusting her eyeglasses on her nose, she pretends that she's Ms. Drumm, and relates the following story from before she was born:

This happened right after my parents got married. They were living in Hong Kong, renting an old house that had been vacant for some time before. Almost immediately my mother noticed that the plastic-wrapped hard candies she bought for visitors and kept in a glass dish on a table in the living room were disappearing. Neither she nor my father were eating them. Even more mysterious, she sometimes found one or two, partly unwrapped, lying on the hardwood floor beside the wood door leading to the cellar steps. Plus she was always sweeping up sawdust shavings in that area.

She told my father: "I think some sort of animal is living in our basement." As it turned out, my father wasn't surprised. For some weeks he'd suspected the same on account of peanuts often being missing from a jar he kept on his desk in the home office he'd set up in the basement. Even stranger were the empty shells he sometimes found in his wastebasket that he'd never put there. He hadn't mentioned it to my mother, afraid of how she'd react. He wasn't wrong, either.

"You've got to do something," she told him.

"Yes," he said. "First thing tomorrow I'll buy a trap."

"No, you don't understand. I want you to go downstairs and do something *now*," my mother insisted. "I don't want a furry creature living in my basement. And, anyway, it knows how to climb stairs." As she said this, my mom was turning the laundry room next to the kitchen upside down. Grabbing what was there, a pair of my dad's sweat socks and a large Turkish bath towel, she stuffed them into the rather large crack between the door and the floor. She didn't like to think of some strange animal, lying on its back, hard candy in its paws, squeezing underneath the door.

Well, my dad didn't like thinking about it, either. A biologist, after all, he knows that rodents carry fleas that transmit terrible diseases. That's why the next morning he bought two mousetraps, baited them with fruit paste, and set them on the steps leading up from the cellar.

Several days passed without anything happening. Then, one morning, as my father was going downstairs to check his traps, my mother said, "Maybe you should try using peanuts instead, or hard candy as bait."

Giving her a funny look, my father asked, "When did you get to be such an expert on trapping?" Since they'd been married, this was their first disagreement. Afterward they both felt bad. That night, hoping to make up, my father took her advice and used peanuts.

In the morning, when he inspected the traps, he found both had been sprung. The peanuts were gone, but he hadn't caught any animal. At exactly the same time my father was discovering this, my mother was making up her mind to remove the rolled-up towel and socks she'd stuffed underneath the door.

"How foolish! There's probably nothing down there. This is clearly a case of overreacting," she told herself. Then, picking up the towel my father had pushed aside, she began to unroll it. That's when she noticed both socks were gone, except for a few bright threads that trailed from the door. Half the towel was also missing, leaving the remaining half with a long, jagged, saw-toothed edge—clearly a sign of some terrible, late-night struggle, my mother decided. Naturally she was horrified. Even my dad was surprised when she showed him.

"I think you'd better buy a larger trap," she told him.

After my father left for work that day, my mother tried hard to imagine what sort of animal could possibly be lurking in the basement; and how had it gotten in? Well, of course it could have started out small, and just grown larger living downstairs. She considered a ferret, or some other weasel.

"But how does it survive without water?" she asked my father when he arrived home that evening with a pair of rattraps. "There's nothing to drink down there."

"Oh yes, there is," he replied. "Are you forgetting our sump pump? To a rodent it's as good as a spring-fed well." Right away, my mother pictured a giant salamander, or maybe a China mink, swimming up through their underground pipe, climbing out in the basement.

Time passed. My dad experimented with larger traps, and different bait. "I'm feeding rats in my basement," he'd mutter to himself when he found his traps emptied and sprung.

"Maybe we should get a cat, or borrow one," my mother suggested, but my dad believes that animals don't belong in houses, living with people. "There's one living in the house with us now. It's only a question of what kind," my mother pointed out. For her part, she'd removed all food from view, and also added to her Turkish towel barricade.

She discussed the problem with relatives and neighbors. "What do you think can be living in my basement?" she'd ask almost anyone.

It drove my father crazy. "It's nobody's business," he told her. "It's always a mistake to tell everything you know."

At last, a widower living next door came to her aid. Monsieur

Jourdan was a retired diplomat who'd been raised in the south of France. He liked telling tales he'd heard as a child. "You know, I think your problem isn't an animal. I think you may have a ghost in your basement," he told my mom one day.

"A ghost?" said my mom. It wasn't something she'd even considered.

"Oh yes," said Monsieur Jourdan. "I once heard of something similar. A relative of mine played a part in it, and it's a true story." Then he told it to her: "It seems at one time a certain Monsieur Vidal died, leaving no family behind. His house remained empty for over a year. The same as yours," said Monsieur Jourdan. "When a family was finally found to move in, they didn't stay very long. It was too noisy there. Every night, just as they were falling asleep, they'd be awakened by strange sounds, as of someone, or something, shuffling around. As hard as they tried, they never could discover where the noises came from. A short time later, they moved away. 'That house is haunted,' said the neighbors. Afterward, no one wanted to live there."

"So, how did it turn out?" my mother asked.

"That's where my relative came in," said Monsieur Jourdan. "He didn't believe in ghosts. He made up his mind to stay overnight in that house and see what was what. He took with him his old army saber, and a lantern whose light he hid behind his cloak. He stretched himself out under the stairway. But just as he started falling asleep, he was awakened by noises, as of someone, or something, shuffling around. Before you could blink, he was on his feet, his lantern uncovered. So what do you think he saw? Just this: three very large rats running up the stairs. No ghost at all."

My mother laughed. "Yes, but why do you think my problem is a ghost, then?"

"Ah, don't you see," answered Monsieur Jourdan. "Stories are like dreams. They go by opposites. My countrymen thought ghosts, but it turned out rats. For sure, your animal will end up being something else."

Thinking it was a funny story, my mother told it that night to my dad. As time went by, however, she thought about it more and more. She herself had always lived in a city, but both her grandmothers had grown up in the Chinese countryside. Like Monsieur Jourdan, they, too, told stories. Some were about ghosts. Some of the ghosts also were tricksters: foxes, badgers, or some other animal. The possibility that such things existed, therefore, didn't come as a total surprise to my mom. There also was this: Though the thought of a rodent in the basement horrified her, my mother is not in other ways a timid person.

That was why, a week or so later, when my dad went to London for a month on a teaching assignment, my mother made up her mind to stay overnight in the basement and see what was what. She took with her a sharp kitchen knife, and also a multipurpose three-way lantern my dad had bought for emergencies. On one end it had a krypton spotlight bulb, a blinking amber beam to call for help, and soft area illumination. At the opposite end was an AM/FM radio. My mom went downstairs and curled up in my father's easy chair to watch.

After some time had gone by, she began to nod, and her eyelids closed. No sooner did she start to fall asleep, however, than she was awakened by noises, as of someone, or something, moving about in the basement. At the same time, she thought she also heard music, and just for a second wondered if, perhaps, it was coming from the radio end of her lantern. Then, almost before you could blink, she was on her feet, her krypton spotlight bulb switched on, and her kitchen knife in her hand.

"I'm armed," she announced in her loudest voice, trying to sound brave, and also to look taller. She waved the knife about in the air and directed the krypton beam along the plaster walls, and into the corners. She herself was blinded at first by so much sudden light, but when she finally could see, this was what she saw: A man was leaning gracefully against the farthest wall, beneath a window well. He was pale and slim, with a narrow face and pearly white teeth, and very good-looking. He lowered the bamboo flute he'd been playing and bowed deeply. That was when my mother noticed he had on my father's socks, and also the missing portion of her towel was draped across his back. She could also see, then, he had long, shiny hair, dark chestnut-red, held back by frayed thread in a ponytail. *For goodness' sake,* she thought. *A homeless man is living in my basement; a musician, no less.* Not knowing what else to do, she tried making conversation.

"How nicely you play," she said to the man. "I myself have never had lessons, but I'm a very good listener. I'm also fond of dancing." Well, she'd been alone in the house all day with no one to talk to. By now, she was ready for a little chitchat, no matter with whom.

"Ah," the man said, and nodded in an understanding way.

One thing led to another. My mom's a hospitable person, not about to put a homeless person out after dark, and my dad wasn't at home to consult. Therefore, she did the only thing that came to mind.

"Would you like something to eat?" she asked the musician. Of course he said yes. So that's how it started. For the rest of the time my father was gone, each evening my mother prepared two dinners—steamed fish and rice, for instance, candies for dessert—then carried them downstairs. She and the stranger dined together by lantern light, set on soft area illumination, and listened to the radio. Afterward, he played his flute, and my mother brushed up on her dancing. She hadn't practiced since her wedding. Sometimes, she turned back on the radio. Then, laying down his flute, the musician danced with her. They danced the rumba and the waltz, the tango and the fox-trot. Once, my mother says, unable to resist, she raised her hand and touched her partner's long, sleek hair. He stopped dancing at once.

"Don't ever do that!" he said, and my mother didn't, ever again.

A month went by like this, until one day it was time for my dad to return. "If I were you, I'd lie low for a bit," my mother warned the stranger. "I probably won't get back for a while. My husband is a very fine person, but, still, I think he might not understand what you are doing in our basement." Somehow it slipped my mother's mind completely to provide any food to hold the musician over while she was gone, and I guess he was too polite to remind her.

The following afternoon, my father came home. He kissed my mom and said, "I really missed you." Of course my mom was glad to hear it.

"What's in that box?" she asked, pointing.

My father unwrapped a large wire cage. "It's a trap," he said. "It's big enough for catching any animal that may have moved into our basement. Well, unless it's a bear. The man who sold it to me once had a similar problem." Then my father showed my mother how the spring-lock door at one end snapped shut when a lever was tripped, and how to release it. A second door at the opposite end fastened with a latch.

Speechless, my mother examined the cage. After dinner, she watched carefully as my father baited the trap with peanuts. Just before he carried it downstairs, she remembered to slip a bit of leftover fish and a piece of rice cake inside. She'd already made up her mind to keep away from the basement. "A happy marriage is better than dancing," she told me.

That evening, she and my father turned in early. In the middle of the night, my father sat up in bed and turned on a light. "Do you hear something?" he asked my mom.

"Like what?" she said.

"Nothing," he said. "I must have been dreaming." I think he didn't want to alarm her with talk of music coming from the basement. Naturally, she wasn't about to mention it, either. They both went back to sleep.

First thing the next morning, my dad went downstairs to check on his trap. He called excitedly upstairs to my mom to come join him.

"My goodness!" she said, staring closely at the cage. All the peanuts were gone, and so were the fish and the rice cake. Both doors were wide open. Lying nearby were pieces of my father's socks, and part of a towel, neatly folded. Also, many long strands of dark hair lay scattered on the floor, as though left behind by some animal in a hurry. They looked familiar to my mom.

"Well, that's that," said my dad. "It was probably a badger, or even a fox. One thing's for sure, it's not coming back. It would be too embarrassed to return without its tail, believe me." My mother believed him.

"At least that's what she's always told me," Aimee says. "Even so, to this day, my mom avoids basements. As for letting me have a slumber party in ours, it's not something she'd even consider."

# Tokoloshi

Back from her librarians' convention, Ms. Drumm can hardly wait to share her new information. "A tokoloshi—just imagine!" she says, interrupting a group of science club students who have actually come to the library to study.

"What's a tokoloshi?" asks Albert, his eyes focused on a book opened to a page containing complicated-looking formulas and numbers.

"That's exactly what I asked when I first heard of one," Ms. Drumm replies. "A conference doesn't go on every moment. Therefore, I saved some time for sightseeing. My first stop was the National Museum of African Art. A folklife festival was going on. Among the artists showing off their work was a Bantu wood-carver. I paused to chat with him and to admire his display, a series of uncanny-looking animals. I couldn't keep myself from touching one.

"'It's a tokoloshi,' he said.

"'Yes?' I said. 'And what is that?'

"This is what the artist told me: 'In Zululand, where my family is from, everyone knows that a woman about to give birth must stay in her house and keep the door closed. This is so if the baby is born an animal, it won't scurry outside. Then the woman's brother can skin the animal and release the baby. This has happened in Africa. It is a true story.'

"'But what if they forget?' I asked.

"'Ah, that has happened, too,' the artist answered. 'Then the tokoloshi escapes with the infant, runs to the river, and stays there, playing tricks on people and making trouble. Of course, nowadays, many people regard all this as so much superstition. They had better be careful, and not only in South Africa. Tokoloshi are forever on the lookout for new territory; and they don't mind traveling. I know of one case that took place some years ago right here in America. It concerned my own relatives. Listen,' he said."

When my sister's youngest daughter was expecting a baby, she was on tour in Indiana with her husband and her brother. Like me, they're all three wood-carvers, and were there to show their work. My niece's plan was to have the baby behind closed doors in the home of a Bantu friend, living just outside Indianapolis, who would also serve as her midwife. My nephew was expected to stand guard nearby, his carving knife close at hand.

Instead, my niece went into labor three weeks early, downtown, on a city bus. Alerted to the circumstances, the driver pulled over at once. Parking his vehicle, he got off, hailed a police car, and helped my relatives into it. Then, with lights flashing and sirens blaring, the officer drove them to the nearest hospital.

My niece was admitted to the maternity ward. Having accompanied her there, her husband and her brother were not allowed to stay. They were directed down the hall and told to wait in the visitors' lounge. Fortunately, along the way, my nephew managed to borrow a hospital uniform from a passing cart. He changed clothes in the men's room. Then, disguised as an orderly, he retraced his steps to where he'd last seen his sister. He arrived just in time to see her being rushed by gurney to the delivery room, through swinging doors that opened readily.

Trying to look occupied, my nephew waited anxiously outside. Soon he heard his sister moan, then shriek, at last call out his name. This was followed by eerie silence—for sure a roomful of people all holding their breaths. Next came sounds of pandemonium: gasps of air being exhaled; shouts and murmurs; orders given; beneath it all, a clicking noise—animal nails against a linoleum floor.

Gently, my nephew pressed on one of the doors, opening it slightly. At once, he felt a small, furry creature scurry past his ankles and saw it race down the hall. In a flash he was after it, following as it made a sharp turn into the nursery where helpless newborns squirmed in their cribs. Unfortunately, my nephew wasn't armed, having left his carving knife back at the hotel, along with his other art supplies. Luckily, lying atop a glass-door supply cabinet was a pair of surgical scissors. My nephew picked it up. Before he could do anything with it, however, the animal leaped into the air and impaled itself on the point of one blade. Just like that, my nephew found himself cradling a natural infant in his arms, a tiny boy, my niece's son.

You can imagine the confusion in that corridor. Everybody told a different tale: "An attempted kidnapping," said one. Another said, "It was the brother who ran off with the baby." "To perform an ancient ritual," a third witness added. A registered nurse insisted she'd seen the infant take off on its own. "Upright and running," a colleague claimed. "I'm not surprised," the attending obstetrician observed. "It's a known fact that African children are often precocious."

Well, the same can be said of science club members. Those gathered in the library, however, have by now abandoned their work. They're eager to hear how the story ends: "So that was that," Ms. Drumm concludes. "Not only did the artist's nephew save his sister's baby from the mischievous tokoloshi, he also kept them from gaining a permanent foothold in this country. That's why, even today, so far as we know, there are no more tokoloshi in America, not one."

Bird-boy

Dr. Proctor, Language Arts teacher, has arranged for his class, accompanied by the new student teacher, Ms. Tucker, to go to the library for a lesson on fables. It's a required curriculum topic, but as far as Dr. Proctor is concerned, that doesn't mean he needs to be the one to teach it. Every year, when the subject comes up, he grumbles to Ms. Drumm, "In college I majored in English literature. I wrote my doctoral thesis on Chaucer. Why should I care about some ancient tales of talking animals? I'm sure you can handle it better."

Ms. Drumm is sure she can, too. For one thing, don't her favorite stories all include furred or feathered creatures, or sometimes ones with scales?

"Come in! Sit down!" she tells the noisy, boisterous class now clomping into the room. She raps three times on the floor with her stick. "Hurry up and find seats," she orders the slowpokes. Those still dawdling, she calls by name: "You, Zina, and Zoë! You, Priscilla!

Leo and Darius! Kirat and Terrell! Miss Lalli and Molly Rose, too! Pay attention! At least *look* interested!" Finally, when everyone seems settled, Ms. Drumm begins her story.

"It's a tale about Crow and a boy named Sam. It starts out in the Dreamtime," she says. "Sam was in fourth grade, in traditional school, when he heard the first part from his Australian grandfather. Among their ancestors were members of the Dreamtime people. Listen."

Ages ago, so goes the tale, Crow was a person, a mighty warrior. As time passed, he grew ever more brash, and arrogant, and cruel. For punishment, where once that grand soldier had stood, suddenly there was only a big, black bird. Crow came into the world that way for the first time, cunning and wary, and hard to creep up on. He's still cruel—destroying and eating whatever small creatures he can: baby birds, young rabbits, helpless rodents. Mostly, though, he feeds on what's dead. He never forgets he once was a man. He watches from treetops, and shrieks curses after people. Some say he remembers the word that would turn him back into a person, but his tongue is so thick, and his voice is so harsh, he no longer can properly speak it. They claim that is why he sits in trees muttering to himself; he's still trying to say that magic word.

Alas for poor Sam. He took to heart only the ending. A well-meaning child, though frequently bossy, he often talked to animals. Now he made up his mind to help the crows. Knowledgable in elocution, a time-honored subject taught in his school, he coached them in vowels: "A-E-I-O-U," Sam intoned. "Now you say it," he commanded the birds.

But the crows only cawed back: "Caw! Caw! Caw!"

Sam tried again. "A-E-I-O-U. You need to stretch your vocal cords and throat muscles; modulate your tones. Practice! Practice! Practice!" he told them.

Thinking Sam was making fun of them, the crows shrieked angrily. Swooping down from their treetop stations, they flew at him. They swatted his head with their wings, and yanked at his hair with their feet. Then they sped onward.

Gradually recovering his composure, Sam told himself, "Perhaps I came too near their nests and scared them. Next time I'll stand farther back." So he did, but it meant he had to shout much louder now for them to hear him. "A-E-I-O-U," Sam screamed at the crows.

"That's a very rude and crude young man. Who does he think he is?" the crows asked one another, even surer than before that Sam was ridiculing them. "That child needs a lesson in manners." So saying, they swooped down again, this time using their beaks, pecking at his face, including his lips and his cheeks, his ears, his nose, and his eyes. Fortunately, Sam closed his lids in time, and didn't wind up blind. Still, it was a harrowing experience. In a huff, he ran all the way home and reported it to his mother.

"Awwh, everyone knows that crows are all caw and no bite," his mother said, thinking her careless son most likely had tripped, fallen into a thornbush, and gotten pricked. "You always want to look where you're going," she told him.

"Pick up stray cats, you'll wind up scratched! Haven't I told you that before?" was what Sam's father said when he got home and heard the story. Sam ground his teeth in dismay. How he hated not being believed! Still, he told himself, perhaps crows just didn't like being shouted at.

Sam's third encounter with them came in the school yard at recess. Priding himself on boldness, determined as ever to help, Sam bravely fastened his gaze on a row of black birds perched along the fencetop. "A," he mouthed upward. Before he ever got to "E," they struck, an enraged crowd of crows, knocking him down, tearing at his clothes with their talons, stabbing with their beaks wherever skin was exposed. Sam covered his body and his head as well as he could with both hands. But it was the frightened shrieks of other children in the yard that at last induced the crows to leave. So much commotion finally caught the teachers' attention.

*I will not lie. I will not fight,* all the children, including Sam, were made to write one hundred times in their notebooks. "Don't think we don't know a tall tale when we hear one. We weren't born yesterday," the teachers told them. "Crows, indeed!" they muttered among themselves.

"Birdbrain," was what some of Sam's schoolmates called him afterward, their fingers cramped from so much writing. Others simply stopped speaking to him. "Even crows don't like bossy," they told one another, blaming Sam for their punishment.

For his part, Sam had learned his lesson. "Be crows, then," he'd whisper, hearing them caw. "Ingrates," he'd rasp, hurrying past them, his eyes to the ground. It's a good way to miss an air attack coming.

The crows bided their time, held on to their grudge, patiently waited for the coast to be clear. Weeks went by when they only shrieked after him, "Boy! Boy! Boy!"

"Gibberish," Sam muttered, and covered his ears. It's definitely not the best way to hear warning signs of a bird bombardment.

At last came a day when Sam was all alone on the street, the other children having grown tired by now of following after and taunting him, not one wanting to walk with him. He'd become a pariah. Meantime, overhead in the treetops was perched a phalanx of crows, guided by an old warrior. This was the moment for which they'd been watching.

First came a single shriek from their leader. Next came the sound of wings beating air. Then, like stones hurled from above, came the birds. They could have been jet-propelled downward, so fast did they dive, assaulting Sam from above and behind, slashing and slicing, wing-slapping him to the ground, his head dashed against the concrete. Not counting the crows, no one was there to hear the awful sound his skull made cracking. In that instant, Sam's soul transitioned into another world, and a host of crows, unknowing, touched down to dine in this one.

Hardly a helping, just a few morsels, and the mealtime was over. From high overhead came shrill warning screeches: two sentinel crows doing their jobs. Joggers were coming, a half dozen pairs of runners' shoes pounding the pavement. A split second, no more, and the birds all had scattered, regrouped in the trees overlooking such carnage. Calmly chattering and preening, they seemed for all the world like any colony of crows. All alone, though, on the tallest branch of an ancient tree, sat that old warrior, cunning and wary, hard to creep up on, still muttering to himself.

"Aggh, how disgusting!" In the library, students are aghast. Some are making gagging sounds. Some are making gagging gestures. Some are doing both. For her part, the new student teacher seems almost not to be breathing. She's *that* absorbed in the story.

"Wait," says Ms. Drumm. "There's more."

. . . . . . . . . .

As everyone knows, crows are mainly scavengers, feeding on carrion, and not killer-birds. DEAD BOY PECKED BY VULTURE-CROWS, read next day's headlines. CAUSE OF DEATH UNKNOWN. Even so, the news media were glad to speculate: incipient epilepsy, sudden onset resulting in fatal fall; congenital brain aneurysm; precocious arterial disease leading to stroke; allergic reaction to bee sting; liver disorder. Only the obvious seemed imposssible. Except of course to the crows, and also to those children who'd been present that fateful day in the school yard—and they weren't talking. They'd had enough extracurricular penmanship to last them awhile.

Well, there was one other. Isn't there always?—that same unsleeping someone who eons ago put everything into the world for the first time. Now, taking pity on Sam, that all-knowing superpower restored him from the world of the dead and returned him to earth—small, proud, and still bossy, but now Mockingbird, who can imitate almost anything: any bird, any person, any cat, any insect; a car, a truck, the hum of an overhead power line, the buzz of a streetlight. Mockingbird learns it all and sings it back.

Mockingbird's memory is excellent in other ways, too. He's never forgotten Crow's attack. He's not about to forgive it, either. That's why, to this day, Mockingbird can be seen chasing Crow in the sky, or nose-diving him on the ground; attacking from above, or below, or behind. It's the reason Crow is always fleeing, changing direction in midflight, interrupting his feeding, sleeping in shifts. And to this day, Crow remains tongue-tied; hard as he tries, unable to say that magic word that would turn him back into a person. And Mockingbird, pleased to be who he is, and able to say everything—doesn't.

# Fish Story

All through the telling of Ms. Drumm's Crow tale, Ms. Tucker, the new student teacher, has been sitting, enraptured, at the back of the room. Now she thinks, instead of becoming a classroom teacher, she'd rather be a librarian. She raises her hand.

"Yes?" says Ms. Drumm.

Ms. Tucker says, "I know a story from a long time ago. It's about a magical fish."

"Would you like to tell it?" Ms. Drumm asks.

"Oh, yes," says Ms. Tucker, and begins:

I had just started school at the International Academy near Annapolis. The primary grades were going on a field trip to the National Aquarium in Baltimore. Two chartered buses were transporting the classes. Unfortunately, on the bus assigned to my class there was one seat too few for the number of people, including three class mothers who were there to help. My mother worked, so she couldn't come.

"Follow me, please," my teacher told me. "You can ride on the other bus." After we boarded, she found me a seat. Then she left. I swung my feet and glanced all around. Some of the children *looked* familiar, but there was no one I *knew*; plus, they all were older, and speaking in Spanish. My class was learning French.

"*Parlez vous français?*" I whispered.

"*Español,*" the teacher told me. After that I remained silent for the rest of the trip. The seat beside me stayed empty. I stared out of the dirty window and practiced writing letters with my fingers on the glass. When snacks were given out—graham crackers and boxes of grape juice—I stuck mine in my backpack for later.

At the aquarium, I rejoined my class. We saw the fishes and the snakes, ate lunch, then watched the dolphin show. Each of us was given a dolphin decal to take home. I put mine in my pocket. Then, before I knew it, it was time to go. My teacher led me to that other bus and saw me to my seat. How I dreaded that long trip home, riding on a bus with no one I knew. I tucked up one foot and took out my snack, left over from the morning.

No sooner had I inserted the straw into the juice box, though, when a voice said, "What's your name?" I turned to look. Seated beside me was an elderly woman with pure white hair, a friendly smile, and a bump on her forehead, as though, perhaps, from a fall. Where had she come from? Certainly I hadn't noticed her before.

"Belinda," I replied.

"I thought so. That's my granddaughter's name, too," she told me. "Her mother is working today, so I've come instead on the field trip." I was surprised to learn there was another Belinda in my school. Also, I wondered why that Belinda's grandmother wasn't sitting beside *her.* Probably, I thought, she'd sat beside her on the trip there. Possibly she'd dropped crumbs, or spilled juice, or kicked the seat—three things my mother was always warning me against. Not to mention throwing up, which was even worse. Securing my snack on my lap, I determined to be careful. I myself had only one grandmother, and she lived in New Zealand, far enough away that we had never met.

"Would you like to hear a story?" this grandmother said. "It's sure to shorten the trip, and make it less boring." Then, before I could answer, she began:

"My granny told me this story. It's about *her* grandfather." Then, interrupting herself, the storyteller asked me, "How old are you?"

"Seven," I answered.

"When my granny's tale began to happen, her grandfather was seven, too. He was almost a grown man before it was through. Listen," she said:

Ages ago, when my granny's grandfather was your same age, his mother sent him to gather rushes, long stems of grass that grow by the seashore. Her work was to weave them into baskets, trays, sandals, sieves, fish traps, and other such items, which she then took to market to sell. So there he was that day, squishing sand between his toes, tossing his head, pulling up rushes in a dreamy sort of way. Well, he was rather dreamy to begin with. Just as he stopped to take a rest, he heard a long, drawn-out, mournful sound, as of someone, or something, moaning. Who could be making such a noise? And where was it coming from?

He made up his mind to look around. He walked up and down in the shivery surf, kicking at foam. Suddenly he found himself looking down on a large, beautiful fish caught in a trap. The fish begged my ancestor to free it. "It's not as though I'm an ordinary fish after all. I'm a magical fish caught by mistake. Release me, and I will be forever grateful and sure to repay you in another life." My ancestor didn't know what to think. "There's no such thing as magic," his mother often told him. Yet this fish *was* speaking.

My granny's grandfather had a pocketknife he'd gotten for his birthday. Now he used it to cut the rushes that formed the trap that imprisoned the beautiful fish. It lost no time swimming off, blowing bubbles as it went. "La di da, and fare thee well, until we meet again," it called back over its tail. My ancestor watched it go. Then he shrugged and said to himself, "Well, that's that." When he returned home with even fewer rushes than usual, along with a strange fish story, his mother wasn't pleased. "Get on with you now. I wasn't born yesterday," she told him. Then, shaking her head, she sighed, and wondered how a mom as practical as she was had wound up with such a fanciful son.

Days and weeks passed. Months went by. Often the boy returned to the sea to pull rushes for his mother, but as hard and as carefully as he looked, he never came upon that talking fish again, or any other like it. Eventually, he began to believe perhaps he'd just imagined it. Then one day that nice, dreamy boy was no longer a child. He was a young man, instead, with a mind of his own. He thought he was too old to have to listen to his mother.

"Don't go," she told him that record wet spring when he was just seventeen, and the annual water festival came around. There would be boat races, outdoor games and contests, music and dancing, fireworks, jugglers and acrobats, fancy food stands, and exotic drinks.

"You'll be coming home alone in the dark and the damp. The ground is drenched from so much rain. The rivers are high. If they overflow, a person could drown. Besides, there's no telling what sorts of wet things go wandering at night. It's much too dangerous!"

But that headstrong son said, "Oh, no! It's an auspicious date for a water festival. There'll be a full moon tonight." And off he went.

What a fine time he had, too: He ate and drank, danced and sang, played games, bet on the races, watched the jugglers and acrobats do their tricks, and stayed until the last firework was exploded. It was very late and very dark when he finally set out for home. The moon and the stars were hidden by clouds, and there were signs a storm was coming: strong gusts of cold wind, rumbles of thunder, and lightning in the distance. Hurrying now, he whistled to keep up his courage. The wind whistled back; then the sounds of thunder grew louder, the lightning struck closer, and huge drops of rain began to fall. In his lifetime my ancestor had seen all kinds of weather, but he'd never experienced a storm such as this one. Even knowing the way as well as he did, in almost no time at all he was turned around, lost, with no sense of direction. And that wasn't the worst of it. Oh, no! Just as he thought he'd recovered his bearings, a wall of water rose before him, then crashed over him, carried him along. He thought for sure he was a goner. At any rate, that's what my granny said.

"So this is what it's like to be dead," my ancestor told himself moments later, finding himself still in pitch dark, surrounded by dampness, yet now pleasantly warm and no longer wet. Soft grumbling noises comforted him; and a steady, reassuring beat, which wasn't his own heart, lulled him to sleep.

The next thing he knew after that, it was morning. He awoke in a field of flowers. Beside him knelt a beautiful young woman. She was humming to herself, and weaving chains of purple clover.

Pinching both his earlobes to be sure he wasn't dreaming, my ancestor asked: "Where am I? What happened? Who are you?"

The woman smiled. "As you see, I'm a human," she said. "But once, in another life, I was a fish. One day I was caught in a trap. A young boy freed me. You were that boy. I promised then that I'd repay you. Last night, I rescued you from drowning. I had to swallow you to do it. I spit you up this morning, as soon as the danger was past. I hope you weren't frightened."

"Oh, no, I would never be frightened so easily." My ancestor was still at that age when he thought being brave was the most important thing. Also, in the time it took the beautiful young woman to tell her story, he'd fallen in love. "Will you marry me?" he asked.

"Oh, yes," she said. "I'd like that very much." So they were married and lived happily ever after, or at least for a long time to come.

Without so much as raising his hand, Louis calls out. "That brave man married a fish?" As far as anyone can remember, it's the first time all term that Louis has participated in class. Out of class is another matter. Then he's been heard to say, and more than once, "That Ms. Tucker is the cutest teacher I've ever seen."

Now that cute teacher says:

That's exactly what I asked the storyteller. "A former fish," she told me. "In her wifely life she remained a person, though she did retain an exceptional ability to swim." Then, before the storyteller could tell me any more, we'd arrived back at the International Academy. The bus pulled to a stop in front of the school. I looked out of the window, searching for my regular driver, and for the yellow bus that would deliver me home. Having spotted them, I turned back to thank the teller for her tale, but she was gone. Glancing down the aisle, I saw only two teachers, giving directions in Spanish, and a class mother. The other children, all out of their seats now, were bending and reaching, gathering their possessions. The bus door was closed. Gathering my own possessions, I was surprised to discover my juice box was empty, and only the wrapping remained from my graham crackers. I certainly didn't remember finishing my snack.

Naturally, when I arrived home, my mother wanted to know all about the field trip. So I told her, including about the other Belinda's grandmother, who'd sat beside me coming back and told me a story. "It was about a talking fish that swallowed a man, then spit him out, and married him. It was so interesting that I ate my whole snack without noticing," I said.

"That's nice, dear," said my mother. She was a bit puzzled, however, to hear there was another Belinda in my school. Having gone to "open house" and every parents' meeting, she thought she knew the names of all the students. "That Belinda must be new," she said.

"Or else invisible," I said. "As soon as her grandmother finished the story, she disappeared into thin air. Maybe they're a magical family."

"Please," said my mother. She thought I was too fanciful. "Dreamy," she called it. "Probably she just went off to find her own grandchild."

It wasn't until later, when I was getting ready for bed, that I remembered my dolphin decal. I reached into my pocket to get it out to show my mother, but my pocket was empty.

"That's too bad," my mother said. "It must have fallen out on the bus." Then, tucking me in, she read me an informational book about sea cows. She was just kissing me good night when the telephone rang. It was her mother calling from New Zealand.

"What a nice surprise! How are you?" said my mother.

"I'm fine now, but I had a very close call, believe me," my grandmother replied. She went on to explain: Earlier that day she'd been trying to cross a street. She'd barely stepped off the curb when a school bus came careering around the corner. "Fortunately, I heard its brakes squealing, and had just enough time to jump out of the way. Unfortunately, I tripped and hit my head on the sidewalk. I've spent most of the day in hospital, unconscious." As upset as she was, my grandmother was speaking very loudly, causing my mother to hold the receiver away from her ear and making it possible for me to hear both sides of the conversation.

While my mother made clucking noises, intended to be comforting, *her* mother went on speaking. "It wasn't entirely unpleasant. While unconscious, I dreamed that I was *on* that school bus, seated beside a little girl named Belinda. How is *our* Belinda?" my grandmother asked.

"Fine," my mother answered. "Go on."

My grandmother continued. "In my dream, I was telling her a story, the same one I used to tell you: about a boy who rescued a fish, and then in turn was saved by the fish, who by then was a beautiful girl. They married, of course, and lived happily ever after."

"Ah!" said my mother. She'd thought that story had sounded familiar. "Yes? Then what happened?" she asked.

"That's about it. Though, I must say, it was rather remarkable how much that little girl in my dream looked like our Belinda. Except she was older." Of course, my grandmother had never actually laid eyes on me, but she meant a lot like the photographs she had, which weren't that recent.

"But are you sure you're okay?" my mother asked.

"Oh, yes, not counting a bump on my head. Still, I can't tell you how queer I felt when I finally came to."

"Well, of course. Imagine, all that time unconscious."

"Yes, but that's not what I meant. What truly was weird was when I awoke I found myself wallowing in graham cracker crumbs, not to mention there was a large, wet, purple place on the sheets, as though someone had spilt grape juice while drinking in bed," said my grandmother.

"You don't say," my mother said, then took a deep breath to calm herself. "Well, never mind. The main thing is that now you're fine. Why don't I just put Belinda on, and you can tell her good night." So that's what they did.

"Good night, Belinda. Pleasant dreams and sleep tight," my grandmother said.

"Good night, Grandma," I said.

A week or so later an envelope from New Zealand came for me in the mail. I opened it and read the letter:

*Dear Belinda,*

*On my way home from the hospital last week, having been treated for a head bump, I found this in my sweater pocket. I thought you might like having it.*

*Love,*

*Grandma.*

I shook the envelope, and something fell out. Upon examination, I saw it was a dolphin decal.

"It was exactly like the one I lost," Ms. Tucker tells the class. No one seems to know what to say. Even Ms. Drumm is speechless.

# Father's Foxy Neighbor

It's late in the day when Stanley and Michael come bursting into the library. They're identical twins, and in the tenth grade.

"Are you here for detention?" Ms. Drumm asks.

"No, ma'am," Stan answers politely.

"We're returning books," Mike adds.

Glancing at the wall clock, Ms. Drumm warns them, "You'd better hurry if you don't want to miss your bus."

"We got put off the bus last week for talking back to the driver. We're walkers now," Stan tells her.

"We're not allowed back on until we apologize," Mike says. "Who cares! We'd sooner walk all year. We're never going to apologize!"

"Well, walking's good exercise, but if I were you, I'd apologize, too," Ms. Drumm advises.

"Why should we? We weren't the only ones who said something, but nobody else got put off," says Stan.

"It's on account of our being twins and easy to spot," explains Mike.
"See, it isn't fair," they say in unison.

"Fair schmare!" mimics Ms. Drumm. "Who cares?" She raps on the floor with her shillelagh to show her displeasure. "You should be glad for the chance to apologize. Sometimes a person never gets to say that he's sorry, and lives to regret it. That's what happened to my father. Listen," she says.

When my father was about your age, he lived in San Francisco, with his parents, and his three much younger sisters: Karissa, Kassandra, and Gabriella. Also, they had a dog at the time, a little fox terrier they walked on a leash. Its official name was Reynard, but Karissa had christened it Zachary, after my dad, and that was the name that stuck.

The house next door to them was rented by an older couple, Mr. and Mrs. Ito. Born and raised in California, Mr. Ito had spent the war years, along with other Americans of Japanese descent, in a concentration camp in New Mexico. It was there that he'd met his wife. After they were released, he married her, and came back home to try to pick up the pieces of his life and start over. He was still doing that when my father knew him.

Before the war, Mr. Ito had been a horticulturist, raising rare and ornate flowers in greenhouses he owned. Having been so suddenly uprooted, though, he'd lost everything he had, including his business. Now he worked for someone else, operating a small coffee shop not far from the bus depot. Nevertheless, flowers remained his true love, and his backyard garden was a joy to behold.

As for Mrs. Ito, what she did or where she lived before the war, I've no idea, but apparently she liked gardening too. In fact, the only times my father and his sisters saw her outside, she was helping

Mr. Ito in his flower beds, or occasionally alone, digging in the dirt, pulling weeds, cutting back shrubs, or watering. Her appearance was almost uncannily youthful, and she seemed by nature to prefer keeping to herself.

"After all she's been though, it's no wonder," my grandmother said, meaning the camps. On the other hand, Mr. Ito was often friendly. Sometimes when he was by himself in the garden and saw my father and his sisters, he'd invite them over to sit on a bench in the shade and look at his flowers, or admire the fish that swam in a pond he and Mrs. Ito had dug. The fish were very beautiful, with long, fancy tails; elaborate fins; and red, green, and gold bodies that shimmered in the sunlight.

"They're called *koi,*" Mr. Ito told them. "They're very long-lived, some say up to three hundred years. Japanese families pass them down from generation to generation. Mine are yet babies. Like you," he said, and smiled kindly at Kassandra and Gabriella.

"Nothing lives three hundred years," said Karissa. My father, too, was doubtful, but said nothing, knowing it was rude to contradict an adult.

"Maybe not in America," Mr. Ito agreed. "But in Japan, things do. Fox spirits live even longer. Eight hundred years, according to Ko Hung, a famous Taoist alchemist who was alive during the third and fourth centuries. It was he who discovered that upon reaching the age of five hundred, foxes can change their form at will into that of a person. Frequently, they go about in the world disguised as beautiful women. Mrs. Ito, for instance, is just such a one. Foxes have run in her family for ages, though some have married ordinary people, like me. But even then, they retain their foxy natures." At that, my aunts' mouths fell open. My father, however, caught his drift.

"It's just a story," he told his sisters afterward. "Foxy can mean more than one thing. Mr. Ito is speaking in metaphor. He's really telling us his wife is not only good-looking, but also clever."

"Yes," said Karissa. "And I think he also means she's truly a fox."

"A foxy fox," chimed in Kassandra and Gabriella.

From that moment on, it became the dream of all three that one day they might become foxes too. Whenever they saw Mrs. Ito tending her garden, they'd go stand by the edge of the drive that separated their properties and stare, as though watching her might offer clues. Seeing them there, she'd sometimes smile, or maybe wave. But she never invited them over.

"Come away," their mother would scold. "You're being rude. No one likes nosy children."

Once, she overheard Karissa explaining to the others, "See, it's because when she works hard, she sweats. She's afraid if we come too close we'll be put off by her foxy stink."

"Let me hear you say that again, and I'll wash your mouth out with soap," her mother told her. "Besides, the correct words are 'perspire' and 'odor.'"

If only Karissa had left it at that. But, no. The very next time she and her siblings joined Mr. Ito in his garden she asked, "Is Mrs. Ito *really* a fox, or do you just say that because she is beautiful?"

Mr. Ito looked thoughtful. Then he replied, "I say it because she is beautiful, and also because it is true. I'll tell you something else. In Japan, it is widely known that foxes make excellent bakers, especially pastry chefs. Wait here for me, please." Then Mr. Ito went into his house and returned with a plate of tiny cakes, each in the shape of a fox and exquisite to behold.

"Mrs. Ito was expecting your visit. She baked these on purpose for you to take home. Genuine fox cookies," he told them. Gazing toward the house, they could just see Mrs. Ito peering out from behind a white cretonne curtain. Her sharp, pointed face was partly hidden by a long fall of dark hair, but her bright eyes and tiny nose were visible. She was waving a paw.

"A paw?" Mike interrupts Ms. Drumm to ask.

"I mean a hand," she says, and goes on with her story:

At home, they sampled the cookies. "To this day I've never tasted anything so delicious," my father still sometimes says. But even as they ate them, Karissa wouldn't quit chattering. "I think she definitely looks like a fox. Isn't that what you think?" Too busy chewing to voice their opinions, Kassandra and Gabriella nodded agreement.

"Stop that this minute! Enough is enough," my father told all three. But, I think, in his heart, he knew the truth all along. That's what makes what they did afterward even more awful. Of course it wasn't *all* my father's fault. It never would have happened had his sisters not kept insisting on his agreeing with them.

"She is, too, a beautiful fox lady. I even saw her paw," Karissa kept saying.

"We did, too! We did, too!" the two babies chanted.

"See, that proves it," Karissa said. I'm told that as children, my aunts could be very annoying.

Finally, to prove they were wrong, my father came up with a plan. "Listen," he told them. "Foxes, no matter their disguise, will always be afraid of dogs; and dogs, particularly fox terriers, will forever know them by their scent, and chase them. Next time we see Mrs. Ito alone in her garden, we'll put Zachary on his leash, take him outside, and walk up and down with him where her grass meets our drive to see what happens." So that's what they did. How could any of them have predicted the terrible consequences?

It was late afternoon, the very next day, when they put the plan to the test. They'd just finished off the last of the cookies when Karissa spotted Mrs. Ito atop a ladder in her garden, pruning a cherry blossom tree. Mr. Ito hadn't yet arrived home from work.

"Here, boy," Karissa called, snapping on Zachary's leash when he came. Then, with Kassandra and Gabriella holding on to it, all four children walked back and forth with the dog at the edge of the drive.

At first, nothing happened. But soon a breeze blew up, carrying a musky odor their way. The dog went wild. Pulling the leash from the babies' hands, and yelping mightily, he headed for the ladder. With barely time enough to take in the scene, Mrs. Ito dropped to the ground, turned into a fox, and raced for her house. Jaws snapping, Zachary ran hard at her heels. Mrs. Ito escaped through an open window, kicking it shut as she went. One bloody paw print remained behind, staining the glass. As for the clothes she'd had on, including a turned-down straw hat, they lay in the dirt until Mr. Ito came home. From the safety of their screened-in back patio, my father and his sisters watched as he picked them up and carried them indoors. For some time afterward, a foxy smell lingered in the air.

For the rest of that summer, my relatives didn't see either of the Itos again. Then, one fall night, as they sat on their front porch in the fading light, they saw both of them carrying boxes down their walk to a waiting cab. Mr. Ito was bent over and looked much older. Mrs. Ito was limping. They never came back. My father and his sisters never had a chance to say they were sorry. They did try telling their parents what had happened.

"It was Zachary's fault. It was all his idea," Karissa said, meaning my father, not the dog.

"It's because she wouldn't stop pestering me," my father explained.

"She let go of the leash! She let go of the leash!" Kassandra and Gabriella said, blaming each other.

Naturally their parents didn't believe them. Their father asked, "Have you children been eating those fox cookies again?"

"Heaven knows what's in them," their mother said. And that was that.


Having finished the tale, Ms. Drumm sits motionless in her chair, her eyes on the twins.

"Yes, but what about the fish?" Stanley asks.

"What fish?" she replies.

"The Japanese *koi* that live so long," Michael says.

"Oh, those fish. They lived happily ever after. When it was clear the Itos weren't returning, the landlord removed the fish and filled in the pond. He gave my father the *koi*. 'No point having them die,' the landlord said. My father was glad to look after them."

"Wow!" says Stanley. "I wouldn't mind having fish like that."

"I'd be glad just to see some," says Michael.

"That's easy enough," Ms. Drumm tells him. "Go on back to my private office. Take a good look at the fish in the tank behind my desk. They are the very same *koi* that were in my story, passed down to me by my father. Well, some are descendants," she calls after them.

It's unlikely they hear her. Both boys are already in her office, staring goggle-eyed at the fish.

"You don't think that story's really true, do you?" they ask each other.

# Haunted House

It's a library sleepover for high honor roll students. "Bring a sleeping bag if you have one, and be prepared to tell a story," read Ms. Drumm's invitation. It's dark in the room, with a single spotlight shining. Only on this one night is food allowed, including exquisite cakes and pastries baked by Ms. Drumm. Marlene is here, the girl with the orange spiked hair. She's wearing her rings, but is minus her gum. She's about to tell a story.

"It's an old-time tale I learned from my brother. This is how he tells it. Listen," she says.

Away off in the country stands an old haunted house. It's been abandoned now for decades. Its last owner, a gambling man from out of state, won it in a card game, then tried to rent it. He never could find anyone willing to stay. Whoever moved in always moved out right away. "That house is haunted," all of them said.

"Ain't haunted, either," the owner insisted. Finally, to prove he was right, he offered a purse of gold coins to the first person who'd spend one whole night in that house.

Now and again some brave soul would try. None ever made it to sunup. By then the house would always be vacant again, and the guest eventually found off in some corner, shuddering and speechless.

In the end some city guy came traipsing by who didn't believe in haunts. "I'll stay," he said, hearing talk of the reward. So he packed up some food, coals to cook it with, an old iron kettle, and a kerosene lamp. Last of all, for entertainment, he slung his guitar over his back. Now he was ready.

When evening came, there he sat, all comfy, on the tattered sofa in the haunted house, strumming his guitar. A nice fire was going in the fireplace, and a brisket of beef was simmering in the iron kettle above the coals. That's when the man closed his eyes, just for a second, only to rest them. In the moment that he did, he heard a noise, a thumping sound, as of someone, or something, falling down. Opening his eyes, he looked around. There, in one corner, was some kind of furry animal, ferretlike, but bigger; much bigger; much, much bigger. It was really big! Way bigger than any ferret that man had ever seen. An urban-dweller now, he'd grown up in the countryside. He knew his ferrets. Still, it had those same pink eyes, yellow fur, and that long, ferret kind of a tail. It also smelled kind of ferret-y. Looking up, the man also saw there was a hole in the ceiling he hadn't seen before, left by a missing plank, through which that thing must have come. As the man gazed at it again, that thing reared back on its hind legs, making itself seem even bigger than before, and said, "Hey, guy, you still gonna be here when Stella comes?"

"Uh-huh, I'll still be here," said the man. Then he got up, added a head of cabbage to the pot, and sat back down on the sofa again. He picked up his guitar and began to pluck it. After a while he grew tired, and his eyelids began to droop. That's when he heard the second thump, a teensy bit louder than the first one; and the musty smell was stronger. This time, when the man opened his eyes, he saw a second something, even bigger than the other, in another corner. It had those same pink eyes, yellow fur, and that long, ferret kind of a tail. It reared back on its hind legs, too. "Hey, guy, you still gonna be here when Stella comes?" it asked.

"Uh-huh," answered the man. "I'll still be here." Then he got up, added a half dozen or so potatoes to the pot, and sat back down on the sofa again. He picked up his guitar and began to play it. Pretty soon, as if on their own, his eyes closed once more and, at the same time, he heard a third thump, even louder than the two before, and that smell was something awful. Opening his eyes, the man saw, landed in another corner, a third something, looking pretty much like the other two, only bigger. Rearing back on its hind legs, it asked the man that same question. "Hey, guy, you still gonna be here when Stella comes?"

"Uh-huh," said the man. "I'll still be here." For the third time, he got up, stirred his brisket of beef, cabbage, and potatoes, then added a handful of carrots and one Spanish onion. Taking back his place on the sofa, he set his guitar on his lap. Only this time he could hardly pick a note he was trembling so bad, plus he was concentrating hard on keeping his eyes wide open. In the end, he had to blink. That's when the fourth something came tumbling into the room, with the loudest thump and the strongest smell so far of all. As big as the other three put together, it, too, reared back on its hind legs, and asked the man, "Hey, guy, you still gonna be here when Stella comes?"

"Uh-huh," said the man. "I'll still be here." But this time he didn't get up to tend to his cooking, or even so much as touch his guitar. Too scared to move, to say nothing of blinking, he stayed where he was, his feet tucked under him. He felt the house shake. Then, in through the doorway this time, came yet another one of those things. It was the fifth one. Its eyes were red, its fur was the color of gold, and its tail was as long as the longest of serpents. Rearing back on its hind legs, it stood nearly as tall as the house. It gave off a smell something like sulfur burning, and every bit as powerful. Not saying one word, it went straight to the fireplace, dipped its paws into the boiling water, pulled out all the food, and ate it. Then, without any holder, it lifted the pot, tipped it over, and washed down its dinner with the greasy water, after which it wiped its mouth on the kettle bottom. You know it *had* to be hot! At last, turning around, facing the man, that thing asked, "Hey, guy, you still gonna be here when Stella comes?"

"Naw," said the man. "Uh-uh! If you ain't Stella, I ain't gonna be here when Stella comes. No sir!" And just that quick, the man was gone, leaving everything he'd brought behind, headed back for the city. "Haunts is one thing, devils is another," he muttered as he went.

Swallowing hard, now, Marlene licks her lips. Her mouth is dry. Then, almost whispering, she finishes the story:

That old house still stands in the country, still haunted. Folk living nearby say that on nights when the moon is full and the wind is low, if you listen closely you can sometimes hear, coming through cracks in the walls or up out of the chimney, a low-pitched, thrumming sound— like the noise that's made by a badly played and out-of-tune guitar. That's all.

· · · · · · · · · ·

Amid applause, Marlene bows. Then, grabbing a cup of juice and a handful of cookies, she lowers herself to the floor.

"Someone tell another," voices shout out in the dark. Murmurs can be heard, and the swish of bodies as they shift positions. Then, "Listen," someone says.

# Snakefeathers

It's Mr. Truehart, assistant vice-principal, and new to the school this year. He's on the short side, and chubby, and he brushes his hair from one ear to the other, hoping to hide his bald spot. Among his duties is supervision of after-school activities. He's never been to a library sleepover before. Now he's suddenly recalled a story that he knows, and wants to tell it. "It really happened, too," he says. "I wouldn't make up something like this."

It was just outside the city limits of Opelika, Alabama, the town where I was born, that a farm girl once fed a fertilized chicken egg to a rattlesnake she was keeping, after which the snake gave birth to a rooster that rattled. Opening its eyes for the first time, that girl was what the rooster saw, whereupon it took her for its mother and followed her wherever she went, including to school.

"Chicken girl," the other children called her. City youngsters, what did they know about roosters? Poultry was poultry to them. Besides, which, they'd always looked down on the girl, her being from the country and all.

"Never mind, I'm sure they mean it as a compliment," the girl told the rooster, not wanting its feelings to be hurt. Nor were they. "Cock-a-doodle-doo!" it crowed, at the same time rattling its tail feathers happily, sounding for all the world like a one-bird-band, both wind and percussion. It was handsome, too, with its comb and its wattles and its spurs all come in.

"That's a fine-looking, fierce-sounding cock that you've got," local farmers told the girl. "Tie blades to its spurs and you'll have yourself some fighter," sportsmen among them advised. More than a few offered good money to buy her rooster.

"No, thank you. It isn't for sale. It's a pet," she replied. "I've raised it from a baby."

"Cock-a-doodle-doo! It's chicken girl and bantam champion," shrieked those other children now, ignorant as ever, but incensed on account of all the money she'd turned down. No one ever offered to buy *their* pets—dogs, cats, guppies, and the like. Scooping up handfuls of pebbles, those annoying children rattled them in mockery. Not satisfied only to ridicule, the biggest bully let one fly. Whizzing past the rooster, the pebble grazed the girl. The bully threw another. Ready this time, the rooster caught it in its beak. Then, in self-defense, and also to protect the girl, the rooster dropped the pebble, rose on its toes, rattled its tail feathers, and flew at the boy. Attacking with its spurs, it also pecked him wherever it could.

"Ouch, ouch, ouch!" wailed the bird-struck boy as he fell to the ground, wounded and bleeding. It was hard to tell that he still was breathing. Soon his whole body began to swell. His face blew up, and his throat closed down. He could barely see, and he couldn't speak. It would be a long time coming before he'd recover.

"Serves him right, too," the country folk said.

Even so, that boy was lucky. The rooster didn't have fangs. That it could inject its venom only so far was the reason the bully didn't die.

The rooster wound up famous. "Imagine, a poison bird!" people from miles around said, even years afterward.

As for the girl, she could have gotten rich by selling her pet, but she didn't. "I've raised it from a chick," she explained to greedy hordes of would-be buyers.

"She was that attached," folk still say in wonder, down in Opelika.

The students clap. So does Ms. Drumm. None of them ever would have guessed that Mr. Truehart could tell tales. Even Mr. Truehart's surprised. In spite of some remaining scars, he thought that he'd forever put behind him all memories of that truly awful poison-chicken day.

# A Conveyance of Lions

It's a routine class visit. Students enrolled in Independent Research 201 are working in the library. They're engaged in a variety of projects.

"My computer is down," Maria announces.

"Mine is, too," says Renee.

"So is mine," says Javonne.

"The whole system is down," Robert informs everyone.

Ms. Drumm is not surprised. She sighs, and taps her stick on the floor for order. "Which one of you wants to tell the rest of us about your project so far?"

Terrell raises his hand. "I will. Mine is about Chinese art," he says when he's called on. He begins reading aloud from his printout:

"Chimera: a mythological monster. Its appearance in Chinese art signifies the artistic exchange that came with the opening of the Silk Route in the second century B.C. In China, winged lions and other fantastic beasts guarded tomb entrances as evil-averting icons. They were also regarded as auspicious omens whose appearance heralded peace and prosperity."

"That's as far as I got," he says.

"Sounds interesting," says Ms. Drumm. "How did you happen to choose that topic?"

"It was on account of my aunt Maudie," answers Terrell. "She's eighty-two, and also a retired newspaper reporter. When she decided suddenly last summer to join an archaeological dig in Xinjiang Province, nearby part of the ancient Silk Road, she put me in charge of her house and her papers. 'You want to be a writer. Consider it an internship,' she told me. Among a stack of clippings and manuscripts she left for me to file was one really weird story. It was written by my aunt in her own unique style: part cursive, part typing. I have it right here." Terrell holds up a thin sheaf of scribbled-on pages for everyone to see. "Do you want me to read it?" he asks.

"Yes," shout out his classmates.

"Please," says Ms. Drumm.

"All right," Terrell says, and begins:

For as long as anyone could recall, the lions had been there, one on each side of the entranceway to the house. Three-storied and tall, the building was constructed of yellow stucco, with a white wood add-on behind, and a circular drive in front. It was modest only when compared with some others in its immediate neighborhood, an odd mélange, atop a long ridge, of mansions and what once had been summer cottages for the rich but were now rented out.

Though I passed by it nearly every day on my daily walk for exercise, other walkers and joggers were the only people I ever saw. I sometimes stopped to admire the lions. Carved from stone, they sat proudly erect on matching pedestals, their chests thrust forward, tiny wings barely visible on their backs. I'd seen flying lions like these in Chinese museums.

Then one day they were gone. What could have happened to them? Not long afterward I found out. How awful!

I heard the story from Earl Munson, a heavyset, redheaded man who'd come with his sister, both of them young and poor, from the hollows of West Virginia to make a killing in the local real estate market. She'd since sold out and moved to Florida to start a business there. Earl had sold me my house, as he'd sold most of the houses in the neighborhood. Hoping one day to sell them again, he kept in touch with his customers, sending Christmas cards and hosting backyard barbecues. I'd stayed away before, but this time I went. Hanging on, shooting the breeze, I waited until the other guests all had gone home before I raised the mystery of the missing felines.

"Do you think they were stolen?" I asked.

Earl's teeth flashed in a grin. "Only in a manner of speaking," he answered. "You know it's a shame, but real estate is a dirty business." He went on to explain. "Over twenty years ago I showed that house to a couple of Japs." Then, noticing my frown, he added, "Hey, you know me. Black, white, yellow—we're all God's people. I love everyone the same. Business is business. Anyway, the name of the Japanese couple is Wang. You couldn't ask for better neighbors—quiet, keep to themselves, lawn always cut, and you know how those Japanese are crazy about flowers."

"Wang? It's not a usual Japanese name. Sounds more Chinese," I said.

"I bet you're right," said Earl. "Come to think of it, they had one of those Chinese dogs, whatta ya call them?"

"Chow?" I prompted.

"Yeah, that's it. That's why they couldn't find an apartment—no pets allowed. That dog was old. 'You could put it to sleep,' I told them. I might as well have been talking about a baby. 'Ever think of renting a house?' I asked them. City people, down from New York on account of government jobs, they hadn't. At the time, my sister in Florida owned that house they're living in now. I was handling it for her. She'd bought it as an investment, then the bottom of the housing market fell out. Until prices recovered, I figured she'd be glad for tenants, even a Jap couple with a Chow. I saw myself as being in a position to do them a favor.

"I took the Wangs by. Funny, isn't it, what attracts people to houses? They fall in love with the tiles, or the tub, or the roof, or the kitchen. Doggone if those Wangs didn't fall in love with the lions.

"Ten days later they moved in. At first they rented on a month-to-month basis, then with a lease and an option to buy. By the time they exercised the option, the Chow had died. I think it was the lions, not the house, they couldn't bear to part with. 'Good pets,' Mr. Wang told my sister at the closing. 'You can go away and not worry who will walk or feed them.'

"Last month they mailed my sister the final payment. I delivered the deed. Mrs. Wang insisted I come inside for cookies and tea. 'Even the lions are celebrating,' she said, pointing to the red ribbons she'd hung around their necks. 'After all, it's their house, too. If not for them we'd probably never have bought it.'

"Mr. Wang laughed. 'Expensive lions if they're what we've been paying for all these years,' he said.

"'Well, you got yourself some nice house in the bargain. When you're ready to sell, we'll both make money,' I told him.

"A week or so later I was in my office when I got a frantic call from Mr. Wang. Two men in a truck had pulled up to his house, and driven off with the lions."

"Stolen?" I asked.

"Not exactly," said Earl. "They had papers."

"The lions?"

"The men." He went on to explain: "The Wangs were eating lunch in their kitchen when they heard loud noises coming from the street. They went to the door to look out. A moving truck was parked in their driveway, and two men were unloading ropes and hoists and an elevator dolly. 'Aiiyee!' shrieked Mrs. Wang. 'Bandits—in broad daylight, no less.' Just as she was deciding whether they should hide, or bang pots and scare the robbers away, the men began tying up the lions with rubberized chains.

"Mr. Wang shouted: 'Hey! Stop! What do you think you're doing?' He unlocked the door and stepped out, Mrs. Wang right behind him.

"'We've got orders to move these lions,' one of the men said.

"'Orders from whom?' asked Mr. Wang.

"'There must be some mistake. The lions are ours,' Mrs. Wang told them.

"'Not according to these papers,' said the other man. He handed Mr. Wang a folder of official-looking documents. By the time Mr. Wang called me, he'd finished reading them, and both lions were in the truck and on their way to Florida. Mrs. Wang was lying in bed with a headache.

"'Calm down. It could be you're getting all worked up over nothing,'

I told him. I promised to pull his contract and see what was what. Swear to God, my heart sank when I read it. When it comes to business, that sister of mine is one smart cookie. How I hated being the one to break the news. But what else could I do? I telephoned Mr. Wang.

"'Bad luck,' I said. 'The lions didn't convey.'

"'Didn't what?' asked Mr. Wang.

"'Convey—like the washing machine did, and the dryer. Remember? They came with the house.'

"'They stopped working almost right away. We replaced them years ago,' said Mr. Wang.

"'Well, yes, but that's neither here nor there,' I told him. 'The point is, the lions remained the seller's property. It says so right here in the contract.' I was looking at it as I spoke.

"'Right where?' asked Mr. Wang, who at the same time, on the other end, was looking at his own copy.

"'Final paragraph, two sentences from the last one.' I read it to him: 'All furnishings, decorations, and other movable items not heretofore specified by name remain the property of the seller and do not convey. See, the lions were never named,' I told him.

"'We named them: Feng and Peng. They were the main reason we bought the house. To my wife, they're almost like children,' said Mr. Wang.

"How sad," Earl said now, looking at me and shaking his head. "But, you know, people are like that. First they sign; later on they ask questions. That's how lawyers make money, isn't it?"

By the time I left Earl's, a full moon had risen and stars filled the sky. The streetlights were on. I couldn't get the lions out of my head.

That night, and for several nights after, I dreamed of them: two winged avatars, restless and glowering, in front of a sprawling Florida mansion that arose, improbably, out of a swamp, and belonged to a tall, thin woman who looked remarkably like Cruella de Vil in the Disney film *101 Dalmations*. One time I was awakened by a wild din. Disoriented, I couldn't decide whether it was the roaring of lions in my dream, or the love calls of neighborhood cats.

The following week, passing by the Wangs' house on my walk, I saw that the lions were back. Huh! How could that be? Not wanting to attract attention, I paused only briefly and stared from the street. The lions looked about the same—maybe thinner. Their wings seemed more protrusive now; their mouths were open. Had they been closed before? I couldn't be sure. The lions I'd seen in my dream had mixed me up. Besides, wasn't it possible that the Wangs had bought a new pair, leaner and meaner-looking than the old ones?

As soon as I got home I telephoned Earl. A voice I didn't recognize told me he'd taken a terrible fall. "A freak accident," she said, and went on to explain: The previous week, reaching for the phone, Earl had slipped in the shower, hit his head on the marble floor, and now lay paralyzed from the neck down in Sibley Hospital. He was in intensive care; no visitors allowed. How shocking! It's the sort of thing that happens every day, but not to people one knows. It drove all thoughts from my mind of the Wangs and the lions.

If not for the Internet, that might have been that. However, the next evening, in an ongoing effort to improve my skills, I was surfing the Web when I came across the following story from a Florida paper:

July____, 20____ Broward County: Sheryl Brawley, local real estate tycoon, found dead in her bed, her body gruesomely mauled as though by wild beasts. According to the police, it's believed she died from natural causes, and that her corpse was then found and chewed on by hungry animals, possibly a pair of Doberman pinschers kept by Ms. Brawley to guard the premises. The dogs are now at the Broward County animal shelter, where they are being held for observation. The police were called to the scene by an on-site groundsman after spotting the mutilated body through an open bedroom window. The groundsman was taken in for questioning but has since been released. Interviewed on television, he said: "I'll eat my shirt if those gashes I saw were made by dogs. A swamp monster, maybe; a cougar, perhaps—or some other wildcat. Only God knows what lives in those Everglades."

I downloaded the article, along with a small inset photo that I then enlarged. It was of the Brawley mansion, taken from the far end of the driveway. Barely visible on each side of the entranceway was a faded, flattened patch of lawn, as though something had recently rested there—a stone pedestal, for instance. How eerie!

Once a reporter, always a reporter! As soon as I heard Earl was receiving visitors, I went by the hospital to see him. Propped up in bed, he remained quadriplegic, unable to do anything for himself except speak. "Darnedest thing," he said. "I was just stepping out of the shower to answer the phone when I heard a weird noise, like wind whooshing by. Wife must have left the skylight open, I thought. That's when I felt a hard swat to the back of my head. It knocked me down. Next thing I know, I awoke in the hospital with a splitting headache, unable to move. 'Could be an aneurysm,' they said, and ran tests. Now they insist that *first* I slipped, *then* banged my head. No one believes me."

I believed him. "They weren't there; you were," I said.

"Right," said Earl. "Worst part was, the call I was reaching for was from Florida to tell me my sister Sheryl was dead. No way could I make it to her funeral."

"I'm so sorry," I said.

"Yes, well, at least she passed peacefully in her bed."

Let him think what he likes, I told myself. It's not my job to enlighten him. I leaned closer to tell him good-bye. That's when I saw it: Exposed by a bald place at the back of his head where his hair had been shaved was a black-and-blue bruise, a sizable blob trailing five smaller ones—for all the world like a Chinese splashed-ink painting of a lion's paw. Oh, my!

Terrell stops reading and lays down his papers. "My aunt Maudie's story ended there, but I wanted to know more," he tells the class. "The next day I looked up the Wangs in the phone book and bicycled to their house. There were the lions in front, exactly as my aunt had described them: sitting up proudly, chests thrust forward, tiny wings barely visible on their backs. I rang the doorbell. It was answered by a small, elderly man; an even smaller, elderly woman stood behind him. 'Hi,' I said. 'I'm an art student, house-sitting for my aunt.' I held out my pencil and pad. 'Would you mind if I made a quick sketch of your lions for art class?'

"'I'm not minding, but better lions elsewhere,' replied the man, clearly reluctant.

"'Nothing special about these,' said the woman. Then, going back inside, they closed the door. At least they hadn't said no. I looked at both statues carefully. I walked all around them, drawing as I went. I examined their heads: stone coils for manes; raised wedges for ears; large, watchful-looking eyes; round nostrils; mouths slightly open; lips pulled back, long canines visible. How godly they looked. I'd love them, too, if they were mine. Then I noticed something odd: The corners of their mouths were smoother and paler than the surrounding stone; a bit worn down. They looked recently scrubbed. Bending closer, I could see the scrubbing had not been entirely successful. Here and there dark speckles clung to their lips and their gums, small blackened spots like dried blood. I gasped and lowered my gaze, taking in the lions' front paws. Entwined in the half-sheathed claws of the one nearest to the right of the door, I saw several strands of red hair. What choice did I have except to believe they were human, and could have come only from Earl Munson's head? *Wow!* I thought; wait until Aunt Maudie hears about this.

"That night I wrote her a letter, addressing it to her last known address in China. Not wanting her to think I'd flipped altogether, I closed it by saying: 'I realize chimera are imaginary beings, with imaginary wings, and that stone statues can't fly.'

"How astonished I was a few weeks later to receive an e-mail reply. It came from Beijing University, Department of Physical Sciences, where it turned out my aunt was now a student." Glancing down at his papers, Terrell picks out one and reads it. It's his aunt Maudie's response:

*The older I grow, the more I realize how much I don't know. This I believe, however: Physical phenomena, regardless of category, are ultimately explainable by scientific principles. Consider this: All matter is made up of moving parts: molecules composed of atoms containing electrons, protons, and neutrons; subdividable into elementary particules and hedrons, including leptons, quarks, baryons, and mesons; universally held together by electric and chemi-*

*cal bonds. Knowing this, isn't it a wonder that anything on earth ever stays in one place? Trust all is well with you. Returning soon.*

*Love,*

*Aunt Maudie*

"And that's what got me hooked on Chinese art," concludes Terrell. Amidst the noise of his classmates' applause comes the sound of beeping computers. The system has come back up.

"Good," says Taslima. "Maybe now I can finish *my* project."

"The modern escalator provides an efficient way of transporting large numbers of people from one level to another at a controlled and even rate. In its most basic form it consists of a series of individual steps mounted on double sets of rods and wheels between two endless chains, moving upwards or downwards within a rigid steel truss frame. Escalators are commonly found in train stations, airports, department stores, and office buildings. . . ." (*The Illustrated Encyclopedia of Science and Invention*, complete in one volume, Nashville, Tennessee: Saltmarsh and Co., 1993)

Mechanical means for relocating people within enclosed spaces is the topic of Taslima's independent research project. Unfortunately, no sooner has she printed out the escalator part when the computer system goes down—again. Some students whine; others turn to Ms. Drumm. "It's going to be like this all day. Why don't you tell us a story? Please!"

"I could do that," Ms. Drumm says. Then, reading over Taslima's shoulder, she adds, "It's a story about an escalator—and a boy named Jimmy. Listen."

Almost every day Jimmy was the last child to be picked up from Kids Care Day Camp. His foster mom worked late, and usually arrived in a rush and out of breath.

"Let's get a move on, Jimmy," she'd say. "We're running late. No time to dawdle." Then she'd grab his hand and take off, headed for the nearest metro stop, three blocks away, the station with the tallest escalators.

"Stand to the right. Hold on to the handrail. Moving steps are dangerous. I could tell you stories," she warned him harshly every time.

"Who cares? She's not my real mom. She's only looking out for me on account of she gets paid," Jimmy told himself. He preferred it that way. Young as he was, already he knew it didn't do to get attached. Any day the lady from social services could come and snatch him away, deposit him someplace else, with some other mother. So for some time, this was the way things stood.

Then came one especially hot Monday in August when the train was late. Underground, in the station, Jimmy's foster mom waited impatiently, stared toward the track, and tapped her foot. Jimmy stood leaning against the metal wall that ran from the escalator handrail to the floor. He pressed an ear against its coolness. That's when he heard it: a sort of humming. Swiveling his head, he listened with his other ear. *Oh, my goodness!* he thought. It sounds like cats miaowing. Kittens, maybe. Funny I never noticed it before. He listened some more, wondering how kittens could have gotten in—and how would they get out? He examined the escalator closely. So far as Jimmy could tell, the space that lay beneath the moving steps was entirely enclosed, by a metal wall on one side, a tile wall on the other.

He tugged at his foster mom's sleeve. "Do cats live inside the escalator?" he asked.

"Cats? I don't think so," she said.

"Then what's making that noise?" Jimmy asked.

Stepping back from the track, his foster mom tilted her head and listened. "Well, you're right about one thing. There's certainly something in there that's humming. Let's hope it's not rats." Then, straightening, she added, "Probably it's just the machinery."

"Oh," Jimmy said. But he knew for a fact that machines don't miaow. "Cats," he said, under his breath, positive now, and happy to know it. Jimmy loved cats. He admired their independent ways. Often, he saved food from his plate to feed local strays.

Catching him at it, his foster mom scolded. "You wouldn't do that if you had to earn your own living. Besides, it's a bad business—feed one, and more come." Longing for a pet as he did, and hoping she was right, Jimmy kept on feeding them. So you can imagine how excited he was now to hear so much miaowing all in one place. Also worried. What did these escalator cats eat? Where did they find water? How did any fresh air ever make its way down there, beneath the moving steps? That Monday, traveling home on the train, Jimmy made up his mind: He'd have to rescue them was all. But how?

For the rest of the week, Jimmy considered the situation carefully. Riding the escalator, he kept his eyes on the stairs. On Friday, he told himself, "Of course I could. It wouldn't be much different from prying up a jelly jar lid. A person only needs the right equipment." At home, stored in his foster mom's cellar, were piles of equipment.

"It's Jack's," his foster mom had told him. "He left it here. It's how I know he's coming back." Having never met Jack, and with no idea who he was, Jimmy could only take her word for it. But in the meantime, he reasoned, Jack was not about to miss some old prying tool borrowed from the basement. Therefore, that night, Jimmy took from one of the piles the shortest crowbar he could find and hid it beneath his mattress, alongside a flashlight he kept there.

He waited until Sunday, the one day his foster mom slept late. She was a Seventh-Day Adventist who attended church on Saturdays. Then, before even the sun was up, Jimmy slipped from his bed and dressed quickly. Wrapping his jacket around the crowbar and putting the flashlight in his pants' pocket, he tiptoed from the house.

He walked to the station, climbed over the gate while no one was watching, descended the not-yet-turned-on stairs to the platform, and waited for the first train of the morning. This early in the day, he had the car to himself. Getting off at the Kids Care stop, he saw only one other person. He waited for her to exit the station before stepping onto the escalator. It was a long ride to the top, giving him plenty of time.

Bending down, he applied the flat end of the crowbar to the bottom edge of the step ahead of him. It wasn't easy. It took several tries. Afraid of being caught, he stopped every few seconds to look around. But at last, halfway past the middle of the ride, the stair popped up, and Jimmy stepped down, pulling it back into place behind him.

Ooooh, it was dark! How glad he was to have brought his flashlight. Turning it on, and maneuvering carefully, he settled himself on an upside-down step returning to the bottom, and again went to work with his crowbar. This time the work went faster. For one thing, by now he'd had practice. Also, hidden from view as he was, he didn't need to keep looking over his shoulder. Then again, who knows?

Maybe the step he'd picked was already loose. Good luck happens sometimes! In any event, almost immediately, the step came up and Jimmy dropped through the opening, crowbar, flashlight, rolled-up jacket, and all. Fortunately, the jacket cushioned his fall, or he might have broken every bone in his body. Instead, he landed unhurt on what seemed to be a giant slide. That's when he nearly became a human toboggan. It was only the pair of no-skid, rubber-soled running shoes he had on that saved him from slipping. Making use of his flashlight, he could see that the step he'd pried up had closed above him, and that the incline he now was kneeling on was made up of metal plates, laid together edge to edge. He used his crowbar one more time.

Finally, his foster mom's warning proved true: Playing on escalators is definitely dangerous. No sooner had the metal plate come up than Jimmy lost his balance, plummeting through the opening he'd made, into a huge and cavernous room that lay beneath the escalator frame. The room was semi-illuminated by light from outside coming in through air vents located high on the walls. Luckily, having landed on a pile of burlap bags, Jimmy escaped so much as a fracture. Still, the impact was sufficient to knock him out completely, and also caused his shoes to fly off his feet, which were sockless.

Young and strong-headed, though, as he was, it was only moments before he came to, awakening to the pleasurable sensation of a pedi-massage. Raising his head, looking down toward his toes, he saw that licking his feet and rubbing against them was a large, very large, in fact a humongous, orange-striped cat. At the same time, it was purring loudly. In a corner, a litter of kittens was mewing. These were precisely the sounds Jimmy had heard from above.

"Ah, so it's you," he said happily. Now he could tell there was no reason for worry, nor felines to rescue—only a noisy family of escalator kittens, cozy at home with their mom. She licked them all, and fed them warm milk, including Jimmy, who'd had nothing at all to eat yet that day. He sighed, satisfied. Down here, underground, it seemed to him was everything a cat, or a person, might ever need.

As time went by, the truth of this was amplified. Certainly, food and drink were plentiful. Hot dogs, shish kabobs, popcorn, gyros, honey-coated roasted nuts, soda pops, orangeade, bottled water, and more—all were fetched from kiosks above by the escalator cat, and offered to Jimmy. From those same stands came a daily supply of clean T-shirts. Also, day by day, Jimmy was able to understand more and more of feline-talk and to communicate with his new family. Plus he found his night-vision had improved, so he didn't mind when his flashlight batteries finally stopped working.

"When you're ready, I'll teach you the ins and the outs of the system," his escalator mom promised. "Then you can come and go as you like."

"Thank you," Jimmy said, as ever, polite. But when it came to going, he knew he'd *never* be ready. Hadn't he spent a whole life time in searching? Didn't he finally have what he'd always longed for: a family of his own, a loving mother who looked after him without being paid, and no social services person to come snatch him away? Why wouldn't he want to stay here forever? He did.

Ms. Drumm pauses to catch her breath—or maybe to consider what comes next.

"What happened to him in the end?" Taslima wants to know.

"Ah," says Ms. Drumm. "Who says it's ended? Go find yourself an open escalator—take a look! Maybe you'll get lucky."

· · · · · · · · · ·

See, it's the same boy, only older. Sunlight coming in through the vents has given him stripes, and time has grown both his hair and his nails. His voice is high-pitched, and he speaks in odd bursts of intonated squalls. Stepping softly, he keeps to the shadows. He knows all the ins and the outs of the underground system, and moves about as he likes. Tired, he takes naps on the floor, curled up like a cat. Watch him, now, as he wakens, rises gracefully, stretches his limbs, and yawns. He tests his nails against the concrete wall. Then, just like that, he's gone.

Before anyone listening even can gasp, the changing bell sounds, and gone, too, is the class.

# Beauty and the Serpent

It's the last day of school. Outside, on the east lawn, the annual school picnic is going on. Picnic tables have been set up and laid out with all sorts of good food: fried chicken; barbecue; potato, macaroni, and other salads. There are green beans, corn on the cob, sliced tomatoes, soda pop, lemonade, and plenty of ice. Everyone seems to be here: Marlene, Taslima, José and Joseph, Stanley and Michael, Jolie, Selinda, and Aimee, all the science club and independent research students, along with Dr. Proctor and his whole noisy class. Others present include Ms. Hall, Mr. Truehart, and that cute student teacher, Ms. Tucker.

Naturally, Ms. Drumm is here too. She's sitting on a low granite bench enjoying the shade of a willow tree. Her shillelagh is propped alongside her. Lazy from the heat, and also from so much eating, students sprawl at her feet and beg her to tell them a story. Ms. Drumm seems to think it over. Then, "School's out! Why not?" she says. "I'll tell you the tale of Bathsheba, a girl your age, and how she fell in love with a snake handler, married him, gave birth to a daughter named Beauty, then undertook a journey to try to change her destiny. It's a cautionary tale. Listen."

Born to upright, hardworking, churchgoing parents in Georgia, Bathsheba was named for King David's favorite wife, mother of Solomon, and was taught from infancy always to walk in righteousness and praise Jesus. Until midway through her sixteenth summer, the Lord knows she tried. Then one Saturday morning, as she stood behind the counter in her daddy's general store, without warning, she was love-blinded. Had Cupid shot her through the heart with an arrow, it couldn't have happened more suddenly.

Gunston, called Gun, was the one. A dropout from school, but still in his teens, he came in through the doorway dressed to impress, in an open-neck khaki shirt, pants to match, a wide belt with a silver buckle, and scarred leather boots. "I need number four nails and some rope. I'm fixing up my snake boxes. I'm a handler," he told her, proud of it as he could be.

At the same time, he gave her a long, hard look. He liked what he saw. Why wouldn't he? Bathsheba was beautiful, in the first full bloom of her youth, charmingly self-conscious, irresistibly innocent. She was smooth-skinned and fair-cheeked, dewey-eyed, with thick, copper-colored hair falling in waves to her waist. Never having been looked at that way before, Bathsheba blushed. In that instant, they *both* fell in love.

*A snake handler, praise the Lord!* Bathsheba thought, moving gracefully about in the store, filling his order. Having grown up in snake-handling country, she knew what it meant. He belonged to the

Church of the Lord Jesus, whose followers carried poisonous snakes into church and prayed over them. It was written in the Bible: *Behold, I give unto you power to tread on serpents . . . and nothing shall . . . hurt you.* "It's a religion for crazies," Bathsheba had heard all her life. She'd also heard what the handlers said: "Come Judgment Day and we'll see who's right. Don't want to be standing then in the shoes of the disbelievers."

Ringing up the sale, Bathsheba glanced shyly at Gunston's face. Certainly he looked as sane as anyone to her—and also very handsome, with blue-gray, crinkly eyes, and a smile that turned downward. Exchanging money, their fingers brushed, and Bathsheba noticed his hands. They were large, well-shaped, and strong—no blackened joints or missing fingers, yet, from serpent bites. Bathsheba suddenly found herself unaccountably short of breath, teeth chattery, legs trembling— which no doubt helps to explain why, when Gunston asked her to meet him that evening in the alley behind the store, just to talk and to get better acquainted, she said yes.

Of course she knew it was wrong. Had it been right, they could have met in the daylight. But then they would have been seen. Her parents might have found out. They believed neither in sparing the rod, nor in spoiling the child. Up until now it seemed to be working. Sneaking off to meet Gunston that night was to be Bathsheba's first serious act of disobedience. Once a person has failed to say no, it's much harder to say it the next time. Bathsheba didn't know that yet. She was about to find it out.

What matter the details? Sufficient to say they met that night, and the next, and the next. All the rest of that summer, and into the fall, out-of-doors, under the stars, or in Gun's van, they whispered sweet nothings, hugged and kissed, and loved each other. Before winter came, Bathsheba was pregnant. They had to get married, and did. It was a snake-handling preacher they went to: *What therefore God hath joined together, let not man put asunder.* Not even Bathsheba's parents could come between them now. Instead, discovering what she'd done, they disowned her. "God hates deceitful," they told her.

That same day, Bathsheba moved into Gunston's house trailer. It was forty feet long and ten feet wide, set up on cinder blocks in a cleft in the mountainside, woods all around. To the left of the door was a makeshift porch, and behind the trailer a wooden shed. Inside were snake boxes and aquarium tanks housing serpents, mostly timber and canebrake rattlers, now and then a copperhead. The same as pets, a few favorites resided inside the trailer proper, kept in glass tanks atop a kitchen counter. Though she admired their looks, Bathsheba had no desire to handle them.

In church, though, it was a different matter. There, with everybody praying, singing, shouting, stomping; with the noise of tambourines and drums, guitars, and a piano; with Gunston and others up front, taking out the snakes, Bathsheba would sometimes feel a joyful surge of power, the Holy Ghost come over her, urging her to do it. But each time, she resisted. Face flushed, hands spread protectively across her belly, she'd step to the rear so as not to give in to temptation.

"After the baby comes, then you'll do it," Gunston said. "We'll be a snake-handling family, you and me. And the baby, when he's older."

"What if he's a she?" Bathsheba asked.

"When *she's* older, then," Gunston said, and seemed not to notice that Bathsheba shivered as he spoke. Well, winter was hardly over yet.

· · · · · · · · · ·

Spring came and went. Wildflowers blossomed, then fell. A profusion of bright colors blanketed the hills. Finally, early one morning in June, Gunston drove Bathsheba to the hospital to have their baby. He stayed by her side, held her hands, whispered words of encouragement. Until, "It's a girl," said the midwife, and laid the newborn infant on Bathsheba's stomach. Bathsheba lifted her head to look. That's when, for the second time in her life, she fell in love at first sight, forever.

"Hi, there, Beauty," she said, and in so saying, named her. She looked toward Gunston for approval. Overjoyed, as he was, to be a father; awed, as he was, from witnessing all of Bathsheba's labor, he was not about to say no.

"Call her whatever you like. For sure there's never been a more beautiful baby," he said. Then, kissing them both good night, he left the hospital and drove home, alone, in his van—almost flying. Once inside the trailer, he felt a powerful need to praise God, and to offer special thanks for such a miracle. He did what he knew best: took up his favorite snakes, and prayed over them.

Perhaps he didn't pray hard enough, or maybe his excitement was contagious. In any event, that night Gunston got bit bad on his lips by a canebrake rattler, and died on the way to the hospital, seeking help. That's how it happened that on the same day Beauty was born, she also was orphaned, and Bathsheba became a widow. How awful! You can imagine the tears and the grief. Still, life goes on.

"At least he died in the Lord," snake-handling mourners said at the funeral. Those same words had been spoken when Gunston's grandfather, both his parents, and an older brother also died of snakebite. "It was his fate," church mates proclaimed of Gunston now. They tried to console Bathsheba. "See, he left you this sweet baby girl. She'll be the one to carry on," they told her.

Bathsheba was horrified. Not my child! she promised herself, and made a silent vow always to keep her daughter safe, including from serpents. Within the week, she knew what she had to do: Go north, take her baby away from snake country. First, she needed traveling money. She sold Gun's snakes and snake boxes, the van, the trailer, and everything in it she could. Whatever was left she gave to Goodwill. Then, packing a bag with changes of clothes, disposable diapers, and baby-wipes, she tucked Beauty into a hand-sewn sling and took an overnight bus to New York. Could anyplace be safer from serpents, she reasoned, than a city built on cement? Ireland, perhaps, or New Zealand, Greenland or Antarctica—but why expect her to know that?

God looks after fools and babies! Folks say that in the South. It could be they're right, or perhaps Bathsheba's luck was just changing. In any event, having arrived early in the morning at the Port of Authority, Bathsheba exited the terminal, walked east several blocks, then nearly tripped over a sofa in the middle of the sidewalk. Seated cross-legged on it was a slim, black, straight-backed young woman, her hair wild in a glorious frizz, calmly sipping bottled water through a straw. Piled around her were cartons, most of them open, containing clothes, books, and other belongings. Alongside the curb was more furniture.

"Are you moving?" Bathsheba asked politely, thinking perhaps she'd found a vacancy. She'd already heard on the bus how tight housing was in Manhattan.

"Evicted," answered the woman. Then, pointing to the empty place beside her, she said, "Take a load off your feet, why don't you?" Her tones were clipped and pleasant.

Bathsheba sat and, behind cover of her sling, began nursing Beauty. By the time the baby's hunger was satisfied, the two women had exchanged stories. Eulalia's went like this: Born in Antigua to African parents, she was barely eighteen when she'd come to New York, seeking her fortune. She'd found it, more or less, as an itinerant phlebotomist—going door to door, in rich neighborhoods and in poor, drawing blood from the homebound. "It isn't boring and it pays the rent," she told Bathsheba. Except for the past year, when Eulalia's mother had been sick and most of Eulalia's money had to be sent to Antigua for doctors and medicine. Landlords don't want to hear this. Now her mother was dead, and Eulalia had money, but not enough for back rent.

Sometimes a person gets lucky, or maybe even two. "It had to be God was looking out for me the day I ran into you," Eulalia and Bathsheba would tell each other in times to come. But that day, they were too busy. Eulalia spent it giving a crash course to Bathsheba on how to find an apartment in New York. Of course it helped that Bathsheba looked old for her age. "Here's what to do," Eulalia said, and Bathsheba did it: First she put up her hair. Next she tracked down the rental agent; filled in an application; paid cash up front—one month's rent and two months' deposit, nearly all the money she had. Since she said no to a paint job or any improvements, the agent agreed to forgo a credit check, and to accept her single character reference, handwritten on laboratory letterhead, signature indecipherable. Elsewhere in the city references are verified, but apparently not for a fourth-floor walk-up like this one.

Not much wider than a hallway, with paint peeling on the walls and cockroaches behind them, the apartment contained a long room with two alcoves. In one was a stove, a sink, and a refrigerator with some of Eulalia's snapshots still taped to its door. The other alcove held a Murphy bed, the kind that unfolds from a hidden closet. The bathroom had only a shower and a toilet. Hand-washing and tooth-brushing were carried out in the kitchen. Next door, a West Indian couple kept a pair of fighting cocks, airing them now and then on the fire escape. So long as no one kept snakes, Bathsheba was happy. Signing the lease in her name, she moved in with Beauty. Eulalia moved with them. Bathsheba and some of the neighbors helped her carry her stuff back upstairs.

It was a very good arrangement. The two women agreed to share the rent and other expenses. Eulalia helped Bathsheba find a job, cleaning offices at night. While Bathsheba worked, Eulalia looked after Beauty.

"Why should I mind? I love babies," she said. "Besides, you can't leave your child with just *anyone!* Uh-uh! I tell you, staying home with Beauty suits me fine."

It suited Beauty fine too. Eulalia sang lullabies to her and rocked her to sleep. As Beauty got older, Eulalia told her nursery tales. *Sleeping Beauty* was the real Beauty's favorite.

"How long is one hundred years?" she sometimes asked, trying to put off going to bed.

Eulalia told her: "It depends. At the start, it seems forever, but looking back, you wonder where the years went. Now lay your head down and go to sleep." Until, finally, Beauty would close her eyes, and fall asleep, and dream of a wand-waving, spell-casting wise woman, who looked the image of Eulalia. "Fairy godmother," she'd murmur then in her sleep.

*Godchild,* Eulalia would think, looking down, her heart filled with love for her charge.

. . . . . . . . . .

In this way, the years passed. Beauty grew as children do—walking, talking, asking questions, often the same two over and over: "Where is my father? Why don't I have grandparents?" Sighing each time, her mother answered: "They were accident-prone people who died prematurely. Country living's not what it's cracked up to be. That's why we moved to the city." By the time Beauty started kindergarten, she took it for granted: Hers was a family of three—mother, god-mother, and daughter.

When Beauty began all-day first grade, Bathsheba, too, returned to school. Studying by day, working at night, she obtained a high school equivalency diploma, and then went on to a two-year college. Eventually she became an X-ray technician. She loved what she did: days spent arranging people's bodies just so. "Don't breathe," she'd tell her patients, then snap their pictures. Best of all, she liked saying, "You can breathe now," and hearing their grateful intakes of air. "I'm saving lives," she told herself, and also Beauty and Eulalia. That the hours were good, and the money was, too, certainly helped. It allowed them to move uptown, to a rent-controlled apartment on the west side. Age eight by now, Beauty was enrolled in private school.

For the next seven years life was beautiful—two capable and comely women with full-time jobs, and an only daughter to indulge. If Bathsheba ever thought of it, surely snake handling must have seemed a thing of the past, ancient history. Except for that one time: Strolling at night on Broadway, Bathsheba's arm linked with Eulalia's, Beauty skipping in circles around them, they passed a young man on the sidewalk, his shoulders draped by a pair of serpents. He was offering them to passersby to hold so they could have their pictures taken. "Pythons, nonpoisonous," he told them. "The yellow one's an albino." Afterward, he sold them the photos.

"Please, just one picture," Beauty begged, reaching for the yellow snake.

Catching her by her wrists, Bathsheba pulled her past. "Your father was allergic to snakes. You probably are, too. Don't you ever go near them."

Taking Bathsheba's side, Eulalia said, "Snakes are delicate creatures. They're not intended for handling." So that was that, the only time in all those years that the subject came up or that Beauty didn't get what she wanted.

Ms. Drumm stops speaking. Before going on, she sighs. Then, "How swiftly childhood passes," she says, "though it never seems so to the child. Too soon came the summer when Beauty turned fifteen."

She went with her mother and Eulalia to Cape Cod for a week's vacation. On returning to the city she made a new friend. Two floors above them a young woman from Utah had come to be an au pair. Age seventeen, her name was Selina or Celine or Selima. Bathsheba never could remember which, and Eulalia was no help, either. That Mormon girl, they always called her. She was a body-piercing freak. Less than two weeks in New York and already more rings passed through her flesh than a person could readily count—twenty-two in just her left ear rim and lobe. Others attached to her nose, her toes, her eyebrows, her lips, and her tongue tip. Two interlocked in her navel.

"Does her mother know?" Bathsheba asked Beauty. "I thought Mormons didn't do things like that."

"I'm surprised that baby's mom isn't afraid to leave her child alone with such a crazy," Eulalia added.

Believing herself that piercing was weird, Beauty still moved to defend her new friend: "It's her body, after all. It's not as if she's doing drugs. She doesn't smoke or drink, not even coffee—no alcohol and no caffeine. She says body piercing is an ancient custom, religious, practiced by the Aztecs. They pierced their tongues, then threaded the holes with penance grass. The god called Quetzalcóatl taught them. It was thought to be an improvement over sacrificing other humans."

"Yes," said Bathsheba. "But we aren't Aztecs."

"And neither is that girl," said Eulalia. Nevertheless, she *was* interested in ancient customs. Therefore, the next time she visited the library, she looked up Quetzalcóatl: Toltec and Aztec; English name, Plumed Serpent; god of the morning and evening star; also known as Precious Twin; symbol of death and resurrection; when last seen was said to be traveling east, afloat in the Atlantic Ocean on a raft made of snakes. *It's an old story*, Eulalia thought, and decided not to tell it.

So summer progressed as Beauty avidly pursued her new friendship, and grew increasingly contentious at home. Pubescent infatuation, Eulalia called it. The normal throes of adolescence, Bathsheba hoped. How relieved both women were in August to hear that the au pair was leaving. Beauty broke the news. Naturally, she was heartbroken.

"It isn't fair. The baby's mom won't even pay her plane fare back. Her brother is coming by bus to fetch her. He's staying five days. On Labor Day weekend, they're returning to Utah together."

Soon afterward, on the elevator, Bathsheba heard the news confirmed. "It didn't work out. That girl is too weird," the baby's mother told her.

"But won't your baby miss her?" asked Bathsheba.

"He'll get over it. Besides, I've already arranged for a replacement."

"A replacement?" Bathsheba was amazed. "From where?"

"Utah," answered the mother. "It's an agency that specializes in Mormon girls. I found it on the Internet."

"I see," said Bathsheba.

Now, this moment, the au pair's brother is here, and he's all that Beauty talks about. "Twin brother," she says. "Fraternal, of course, but they look exactly alike." Their first time sharing the elevator with the twins, Eulalia and Bathsheba see what she means. Both teens are tall and slender, with pale skin even this late in summer, and faded blue eyes. They wear their blondish hair pulled back in long, stringy ponytails. Already the boy has a nose stone and a single earring.

"He's not really *that* much into body piercing," Beauty informs her mother.

But the next day Bathsheba and Eulalia see him in the lobby, lifting the baby out of the stroller. He's bent over, and the cropped T-shirt he's wearing leaves his lower back partly exposed, showing off the bottom half of what's surely a cross tattooed up and down his spine. Beneath it, JESUS SAVES is spelled out in brightly inked letters, accentuated by pearls that attach to his skin. As Eulalia stares, Bathsheba looks elsewhere. Outside, she asks, "What's next?"

Eulalia shrugs, extravagantly, and rolls her eyes.

Saturday now, late afternoon. Beauty accompanies her friends to the bus depot, seeing them off.

"At least that's over," Bathsheba and Eulalia tell each other, puttering in the kitchen, awaiting Beauty's return. Expecting she'll be despondent, they're preparing little treats for her: kiwi fruits and shredded coconut, pepperoni pizza, ripe berries. Italian ices are in the freezer. How surprised they are then when she comes waltzing through the doorway, dizzily chattering, and her eyes aglow. Her mood seems euphoric. Seeing her like this, Bathsheba's breath catches in her throat and her heart quickens. How well Beauty fits her name! In that moment, Bathsheba's reminded of Gunston—not only his looks, but also his ways. She can almost picture him, the way he used to be, in ecstasy, coming home from church, high from handling snakes. It was a feverish state that sometimes went on for hours, and that she hasn't much thought of in years. Recalling it now, she reaches out uneasily and touches Beauty's face. Then, pulling back her hand as though burned, she tells Eulalia, "Feel her."

Eulalia does. "Late summer flu," she murmurs, and heads for the bathroom, returning with a cold, damp washcloth to lay on Beauty's forehead, two aspirins, and a paper cup filled with water. "Not to mention so much running around and overexcitement. Here, take these! You'll feel better in an hour."

But in less time than that, Beauty crashes, comes down from her high, lies docile on the sofa, her head in her mother's lap, pale and cuddlesome the way she used to be, when having misbehaved she still hoped to avoid retribution.

Tongue clucking, Eulalia fetches Beauty a fresh nightgown and moves to undress her. She raises Beauty's T-shirt and unfastens her jeans. Then both women gasp. There, in front of their eyes, with Beauty's navel at its center, lies the image of a snake, its coiled body wonderfully tattooed in coral, with black and yellow bands, and brilliant green plumes that form a hood around its head. The colors look wet, as oils newly laid down, and beneath them Beauty's skin is swollen, giving the effect of a painting in relief. Around its margins

Beauty's flesh is tinged with pink. As Bathsheba and Eulalia stare, horrified, Beauty's limbs begin to tremble, and her paleness turns to pallor. Her lips and eyelids swell. Her skin grows clammy.

"We've got to get her to a hospital," Eulalia says as Bathsheba feels for a pulse. Bundling Beauty up in summer blankets, they rush her to the elevator, down to the lobby, outside, and into a cab. They direct the driver to take them as fast as he can to the nearest emergency room. Health workers, both of them, they understand well the twin dangers of septicemia and of allergic reaction.

Please, God, let her live, Bathsheba prays on the way.

Don't let her die, prays Eulalia.

By the time they arrive, Beauty is raving, writhing, soaked in her own perspiration. Both Eulalia and Bathsheba try, but can't make out what she's saying. "Talking in tongues," Bathsheba murmurs, her hands clenched around forms and releases she's been instructed to fill in and sign. She wants to scream: For God's sake, can't you see, this child needs a doctor!

At long last they're waved through the set of swinging double doors. Nurses check Beauty's vital signs, which are slipping. The attending physician palpates her abdomen, including both serpent and feathers; presses her lymph nodes; closely examines her eyes, fingertips, toes—looking for what? Wearily, he shakes his head. Then, stepping away from the bed, he gives orders to a nurse, after which he makes notes in a folder. He tells Bathsheba, "There's a snack bar down the hall in case you want something to eat. As soon as we get your daughter fixed up and in her own room, you can see her. Someone will page you."

Nauseated just by the thought of food, Bathsheba and Eulalia walk up and down in the hallway, instead, holding hands. Whatever each woman's hopes and fears, she keeps them to herself. More than an hour goes by. Several times they return to the emergency room desk to check. At last Bathsheba's name is called. The clerk on duty directs them to a room on the third floor, which turns out to be tiny and windowless. It contains one empty narrow bed, and another holding Beauty. The bed's side rails are raised, though still as Beauty lies, it's hard to see why.

"Is she dead?" Bathsheba asks in a whisper. But, no—according to the floor nurse, she's slipped into a coma, a state of profound insensibility. Hers is a long sleep, deep and unfathomable, that goes on for days and nights and weeks, until, finally, after the third month has passed, Bathsheba and Eulalia decide to take Beauty home.

Bathsheba obtains a sabbatical from work. Daily she bathes Beauty, including the serpent; moves her limbs to exercise them; supervises the snakelike arrangement of hoses and tubes that keep her alive; and prays over her. Daily she's reminded of Gunston, hears God's words on his lips, the promise He handed down through His disciples: *In my name, shall they cast out devils; they shall speak with new tongues; They shall take up serpents; and if they drink any deadly thing, it shall not hurt them.* This time, Bathsheba means to hold Him to it.

As always, Eulalia's there to help. Evenings, she keeps vigil. She doctors Beauty with potions and lotions she orders by mail: African cures from Antigua; Indian medicines from Mexico. She herself goes to pharmacies in Chinatown, returning with powders and liquids. Some of the remedies she rubs on Beauty's body; others she coaxes her to swallow, a drop at a time forced between her dry lips, past her swollen tongue, down her nearly closed, resistant throat. Last of all, she focuses her attention on Beauty's abdomen, strokes the plumed serpent, stares hard into its eyes, and intones secret words as she anoints it with exotic and expensive elixirs guaranteed to make it vanish. Regularly she informs Bathsheba, "It's going away." And as time passes, its colors do seem to fade. "You'll see," Eulalia vows. "Once it's gone for good, Beauty will awaken."

Ms. Drumm pauses. She gazes fondly at the students gathered all around her. Then, like a good fairy granting a wish, she waves her shillelagh in the air and promises a happy ending.

In the meantime, she tells them, Beauty sleeps on. She dreams she's alive; a princess dressed in feathers, sailing on an ocean in a boat made of serpents. It's a long, lonely journey, but Beauty knows that at the end waits a prince. Just as he bends down to kiss her, Beauty awakens.

"Where am I?" she asks. Her mother and Eulalia rush to her side. They try to tell her all that has happened. They raise her nightgown to show her the serpent. How can this be? Nothing is there! Well, there is a slight shadow, the suggestion of an old scar, its shape indistinct now, and also discolored.

"So that would have been that," says Ms. Drumm. "Except thirteen days later, in Georgia, an infant was born with a mark on his torso. It was deep purple in color, and its outline unmistakably resembled a snake, partially coiled and ready for striking.

"'It's some kind of a sign,' said the midwife.

"'It's an omen,' said the infant's father.

"The baby's mother took one look and smiled. 'Gunston; we'll call him Gun,' she murmured, thus naming her firstborn child after a snake-handling ancestor who'd died young. 'He'll be the one to carry on,' she said happily, an avid snake handler herself."

Ms. Drumm sits up straighter on the granite bench. Laying aside her walking stick, she picks up her shawl and, despite the heat, unfolds it and puts it on.

"So far as I know, that's exactly what happened," she says. "It's also true that as that boy grew, so did his birthmark. It's said by the time he was ten, he needed only to flex his abdominal muscles to make that snake dance.

"That's it! Have a good summer. I'll see you in the fall." Rising gracefully, Ms. Drumm walks off. It's amazing how fast she can move leaning on her shillelagh.

At home that same night, getting ready for bed, Ms. Drumm looks at herself in the bathroom mirror. She stares thoughtfully at a faint line that runs across her bare midriff, a streak of mottled skin that could be a birthmark, or maybe a scar. Leisurely, she reaches for a tray of brightly colored eyeshadows she keeps on the counter. Some of them are iridescent. She begins daubing them on. Using the mirror as a guide, she paints a serpent all over her middle. Finished, she admires her work. Then, unable to resist, she starts moving her feet in a sort of a jig. She laughs to see how behind the glass that painted snake is dancing too. How eerie it looks! She'd think it was alive if she didn't know better. . . .

# Notes on the Stories

The stories in this book all are original and have not appeared in print before, with the following exceptions:

"Ghost Story." Typical of ghost tales, variously told, the version here was inspired by a trio of tellings, collected by Nancy Phillips (spring, 1969), and included in *Storytellers, Folktales and Legends from the South*, edited by John A. Burrison (Athens, Georgia: University of Georgia Press, 1989, 1991).

"Basement Imposter." This story originally appeared in somewhat different form in *Hanging Loose* magazine, No. 65, 1994. It was reprinted in the book *He's Sorry, She's Sorry, They're Sorry, Too*, by Barbara Ann Porte (Brooklyn, New York: Hanging Loose Press, 1998). The brief story within the story told by Monsieur Jourdan is based on a much longer tale recounted in *The Memoirs of Frederic Mistral (1830–1914)*, translated by George Wickes (New York: New Directions Books, 1986).

"Bird-boy." The introductory portion of the story about Crow, which Sam heard from his Australian grandfather, is based on a Dreamtime legend first called to my attention in the book *Boori*, by William Neville Scott (New York: Oxford University Press, 1978).

"Haunted House." Based on a widely known and variously told tale, the version here was inspired by one related by Lee Drake, collected by Judith J. Nelson (spring, 1968), and included with the title "When Bozo Comes," in *Storytellers, Folktales and Legends from the South*, edited by John A. Burrison (Athens, Georgia: University of Georgia Press, 1989, 1991).

"Beauty and the Serpent." This story originally appeared in considerably different form in the literary magazine *Confrontation* (Brookville, NY: Long Island University, winter 2000).